Out of Time in the Desert

J. Thomas Hennessey, Jr. PhD

Table of Contents

Disclaimer

This is a work of fiction. Any resemblance to individuals, alive or dead, is purely coincidental. The author makes no assurances that the events depicted happened, as he has taken some liberties with the actual events and individuals involved.

Introduction[1]

Following the Treaty of Versailles in 1919, the League of Nations established mandates for the territories previously occupied by the defeated Central Powers during World War I. The principle was that the territories should eventually become independent, albeit under the tutelage of one of the victorious countries. People in Ottoman provinces feared the Mandate concept since "it seemed to suggest European imperial rule by another name."

At the San Remo Conference in April 1920, Britain received the Mandate for Mesopotamia, known as Iraq in the West, and a mandate for Palestine. In Iraq, the British administration removed most former Ottoman officials, and the new administration was mainly composed of British officials. Many Iraqis started to fear that Iraq might be absorbed into the British Empire.

Discontent with British rule materialized in May 1920 with the onset of mass meetings and demonstrations in Baghdad. The revolution's start was centered on peaceful protests against British rule.

An armed revolt broke out in late June 1920. The revolt soon gained momentum as the British garrisons in the mid-Euphrates region were weak and the armed tribes much stronger. By late July, the armed tribal rebels controlled most of the mid-Euphrates region.

---

[1] *Wikipedia, **Battle of Al-Bawakher, November 2018***

Out of Time in the Desert

The success of the tribes led to the revolt spreading to the lower Euphrates and around Baghdad.

In the battle around the town of Samawah, a small British detachment of Royal Fusiliers responsible for securing the train station was besieged for days. When an armored train arrived to carry them to the main garrison, a fierce battle took place that resulted in many deaths on both sides, and the British detachment was annihilated.

Chapter One: The Platoon

Lieutenant Greg Evans slowly opens his eyes and looks around the small room for his roommate. A slender six-foot blond, Evans looks more like a surfer than an Army officer. The months in the Iraqi sun have heightened his normal tan, and he seems even more like a beachgoing surfer than when he arrived in July 2022, eleven months ago. He knows he is lucky to be a platoon leader in the 82nd Airborne Division. During his two years in the Division, he has come to appreciate the professionalism of its paratroopers and the leadership provided by the noncommissioned officers and his chain of command. The everyday missions that occupy his mind leave little time for anything else. Even though he was a history major in college, Greg has quickly lost interest in the history of the area they are in now.

He recognizes his roommate and second platoon leader, Lieutenant Green, has taken off for morning PT before dawn and has let Greg sleep in.

Greg thinks to himself, another day in Iraq, another day in the sun, and another day to get everyone home in one piece. In the more than eleven months they have been in Iraq, he has only had two paratroopers wounded, and only one of them was medically evacuated out of the country. Specialist Johnson, 2nd squad, has returned to duty as the only one in the platoon to receive a Purple Heart for his wounds. Hopefully, today's patrol will be just another walk in the dust.

Out of Time in the Desert

As he puts on this web gear and grabs his Kevlar helmet, he thinks about how different things are from when he was in ROTC at Cal State. They never prepared you for the tedium that came with waiting for something to happen, but it seldom does. He is sure the Infantry School at Benning tries to prepare all infantry second lieutenants for their roles as platoon leaders. But until you are one, he says to himself, you have no idea.

His eighteen months as the platoon leader of 1st Platoon, Bravo Company, 2nd Battalion, 505th Parachute Infantry, and 3rd Brigade Combat Team have flown by. The eleven months in the "sandbox" have been the best educational opportunity any lieutenant could have. He knows he owes much of the credit to Platoon Sergeant Jeff Sanders. He can't imagine how hard it would be without Sergeant Sanders. As he heads to the mess hall and the morning meeting with Sanders, he now recognizes more than ever that while he, the platoon leader, is in charge, Sanders actually runs the platoon and makes things happen. He knows that not all platoon leaders are as fortunate as he is to have such a strong and capable platoon sergeant. Their relationship has become so close that Greg is comfortable calling SGT Sanders by his first name.

Platoon Sergeant Jeff Sanders, a fifteen-year veteran, has spent most of his Army career in the 82nd Airborne and in the 505th Parachute Infantry Regiment (PIR). He served as a squad leader on his first two deployments, and now, as an E7, he is the senior NCO in 1st platoon. Sanders is on his third deployment with the 3rd BCT, the first in Iraq and the second in Afghanistan. As a seasoned veteran working with soldiers, Sanders has seen five platoon leaders in his ten years with the 505th PIR. He is impressed with Lieutenant Evans's leadership growth and considers him one of the better platoon leaders in the battalion. After more than eighteen months together, he and Evans have formed a strong bond and find their working relationship comfortable and highly effective.

After filling their mess trays with breakfast sausage, scrambled eggs, and toast, Evans and Sanders sit together at one end of the mess tent and review the operations of the last few days. SGT Sanders points out some events that could have been handled differently. He notes that all too often, both SGT Baker, weapons squad, and SGT Jones, 3rd squad, have become too lax in the leadership of their respective squads and remarks,

"I think we need to watch Cory Baker. Weapons Squad is not doing well, and he seems far too distracted."

"He still hasn't heard from his wife?"

"That may be part of it, but he has convinced himself she is cheating on him."

"Jeff, is there anything we can do right now? I know you won't hesitate to act when necessary. Let me know if there is anything I can do. For now, let's review what we need to do for the next few days."

"As far as the rifle squads go, no worries about White and 1st squad. Tim knows his business and is doing a good job taking care of his men. I am more and more impressed with SGT Davis and 2nd squad. I see Ron as a First Sergeant in the future. He will pin on E6 stripes soon after we return to Bragg. Jones, 3rd Squad, is improving, but his troubles with his ex-wife are not going away. Trent is sure that she took most of his savings in the last month. As we know, Corey Baker is not up to standard for a weapons squad leader. I have counseled him on too many occasions for failing to check his equipment, and he is letting his troops get away with far too much. We will have to watch him for the next few weeks."

"Jeff, you always have some good and bad news for our breakfast. Any troopers have problems we need to deal with today before we head out?"

"Lieutenant, you should know that some of the guys in 3rd platoon were harassing Specialist Oldham at chow last night. We know she doesn't take shit from anyone, but this time Booth and Walker took the two 3rd platoon guys behind the tents and taught them a little respect for one of their own. You may want to talk to the 3rd platoon leader later. I don't think his guys are going to whine to him about getting their butts kicked."

After breakfast, Evans heads to the Company Headquarters to meet with the Bravo Company Commander, Captain Charles. Charles is another ROTC commissioned officer who has spent most of his Army time in the 82nd Airborne. Charles was a platoon leader and company executive officer in the battalion before becoming Bravo company commander and knows most of the noncommissioned officers in the battalion by name.

"Good morning, Greg. Grab some coffee and take a seat. What's the latest and greatest news with the 1st platoon?"

"I may have to relieve one of my squad leaders if there is no improvement."

"Baker?"

"Yes, sir. Sanders and I have done about all we can. I expect his marital situation to be a contributing factor, but his performance has been less than satisfactory. If he doesn't improve before we redeploy, I will recommend his relief upon our return to Bragg."

Charles sighs, "Greg, I don't know how he has made it during this deployment, so you do what you believe best. The First Sergeant and I will support your decision. If you think it necessary, we can reassign Baker to headquarters company until we redeploy."

"No sir, Sergeant Sanders and I can take care of Baker for the next few weeks."

"Ok, now let's get down to today's mission."

"This is a straight reconnaissance patrol. First platoon is to scout out the area around the abandoned train station south of Samawah and determine if any remaining Iraqi insurgents have been or are operating in the area. I can't stress enough that this is a reconnaissance patrol. You are to avoid becoming decisively engaged with any enemy forces. The rules of engagement (ROE) remain unchanged: return fire only if fired upon. The company interpreter, Ali Bakar, will accompany the platoon. Any questions?"

"No, sir. I think I have it and will get to the S2[2] shop for the latest intel."

"Greg, accomplish the mission and take care of your troopers. That's all we are asked to do. I think the S2 shop also has current imagery of your patrol area."

As Evans enters the battalion headquarters compound, the battalion colors, with their battle streamers, remind him that his battalion and regiment were the only airborne units to make all four combat jumps in the European Theater during World War II. He muses that it is ironic that they are now fighting sandflies and scorpions more than any other visible enemy.

The battalion S2 section is on his right, and as he walks in, Captain Bronson, the battalion S2, greets him.

"I was expecting you, Lieutenant Evans. Grab a seat at the table, and I will give you what we have on your AO."

After Bronson and an intelligence specialist review the latest intelligence information and aerial photography of the reconnaissance area, Greg notes that the town of Samawah is partly abandoned. The train station to the south is in ruins and appears to have been unused for decades. The aerial photos show that the roof has collapsed and the stone walls have been stripped. There are no rails on the raised rail

---

[2] Intelligence section supporting the battalion

beds that run roughly north to south and east to west. He asks for some of the photos to be printed and pockets three sheets of photos to use with the latest map sheet.

"Are there any reports of enemy activity in the area, Captain Bronson?"

"There have been no reports of recent enemy activity, but that's why you are reconning the area. As a history buff, I know that Samawah and the train station in the center of your platoon's area of operations have some historical significance."

"I'm all ears, Captain."

"During the British Mandate after World War I, one of the larger engagements by the British with the rebels took place in this area. In 1920, the train station and Samawah were featured in a bloody siege that wiped out the British troops at the train station."

"Thanks for the updates and the bit of history. Hopefully, we won't have a similar experience."

As Evans leaves the battalion command post and returns to his company area, he again hopes this is another walk in the dust and no firefights. His unit has been operating out of this Forward Operating Base (FOB) for nine of its eleven months in Iraq. He is reminded how close they are to getting back to the US when he hears one of his soldiers say yesterday, "20 days and a wakeup, and we are out of here."

Out of Time in the Desert

He and Evans meet with squad leaders White, Davis, Baker, and Jones. As Evans goes over the five-paragraph mission order, Sanders looks at the four sergeant squad leaders and sees again how different the four are.

A short, sometimes pugnacious man, SGT Tim White, first squad, is the most experienced of the four. This is White's second tour in Iraq. Solid and sometimes a little too stoic, he can always be counted on to have his squad ready. Sanders suspects that sometimes White doesn't tell him everything about his squad, but his troops are fiercely loyal to him.

A tall, slender black man, 2nd squad leader, SGT Ron Davis is the epitome of an airborne soldier on his first deployment with the Brigade. Sanders knows Davis has potential for future leadership assignments. As such, he often relies on Davis' second squad to be the lead squad in the platoon. Davis's squad is always better prepared and accomplishes its missions. How Davis takes care of his soldiers impresses Sanders every day.

Unfortunately, he doesn't hold either Baker or Jones in such high esteem. For both Baker and Jones, this has been their first deployment in Iraq. Both have their problems. Baker has financial issues with an ex-wife that are unresolved. Jones hasn't heard from his wife in a week and is convinced she is cheating on him. Both sergeants' problems have impacted their performance, and it is apparent to Sanders that their issues are never far from their minds. How much of that is due to their problems and how much is due to their incompetence is yet to be determined. The eleven months away from Ft Bragg haven't helped their problems.

After LT Evans outlines the mission and goes over the area of operation, each squad leader reviews their squad's readiness and how they will execute the mission. They summarize what they have learned about the patrol area and how they will respond if engaged by hostile fire. Their reports on their squads include the status of each soldier, their equipment, and any limitations. Again, Davis is clear and concise. White reviews the mission and confirms his squad is geared up and ready to go. Baker and Jones are less articulate in their review. The weapons squad, Baker's responsibility, is less prepared than the other three, and one of his M60 machine guns should probably be in maintenance.

Evans leaves Sergeant Sanders and the squad leaders to do a final check of their soldiers before departing from the FOB at 1000. While they do not expect to be gone more than 12 hours, each man carries two-day rations, three quarts of water, and more than 300 5.56mm rounds for their M4s. The heavy machine gunners have 1000 7.62mm rounds for their M60s. The three soldiers carrying the light machine gun, M249, have 800 5.56mm rounds for each weapon. The three designated marksmen from each squad have 200 7.62mm rounds for their M110 sniper rifle. The three riflemen with the M320 grenade launchers mounted are carrying sixty rounds between them.

Platoon Sergeant Sanders assembles the platoon of 38 soldiers for LT Evan's final brief.

Out of Time in the Desert

"This is a reconnaissance mission only. The rules of engagement remain unchanged. We fire only if fired upon. We will move to our drop-off location, head west, and then north to our recon area. Once in the platoon's recon area, each rifle squad will do a three-kilometer out and back. 1st squad north, 2nd squad east, and 3rd squad west. Once we arrive, Platoon headquarters and weapons squad will be in the vicinity of the abandoned train station. Any questions?"

"If not, squad leaders take charge of your squads and mount up."

"Burton, one final commo check with the company."

"Roger, done, five by, sir."

Heavily loaded and accustomed to the monotony of travel outside the wire, the soldiers climb into the waiting armored transport vehicles. Third squad members, Bozeman and Walker, now crammed into the personnel carrier, adjust their weapons and equipment for the ride.

"Just another hurry up and wait patrol, eh, Walker?"

"Bozeman, if you can get that long rifle out of my side, this might not be a bad ride."

"Hey, SGT Jones, how long are we going to be stuck in the tin can?"

Don't sweat it, Bozeman. We will get there when we get there."

While each soldier hopes this will be an uneventful patrol, they know to expect the unexpected in this part of Iraq.

Chapter Two: On Patrol

The convoy of five vehicles carrying the platoon travels along a cart path that follows the Euphrates River and the raised railroad bed. The engineers swept the road for IEDs first thing that morning. Evans notices that the rails are long gone and wonders how the locals used those long pieces of steel.

Evans checks his GPS and map and estimates they are about twenty kilometers from the southern part of Samawah. The designated dismount point is coming up, and on the platoon radio net, he calls,

"1-1, 1-2, 1-3, 1-4 dismount. Establish a perimeter as briefed."

The soldiers quickly dismount from the armored personnel carriers and establish a hasty perimeter as the vehicles turn around.

As the armored transports return to the FOB, Evans and Platoon Sergeant Sanders deploy 1st Squad, SGT White, in the lead with 2nd Squad, SGT Davis, on the left flank and 3rd Squad, SGT Jones, on the right flank. The weapons squad, SGT Baker, and the platoon headquarters element of Evans, RTO Burton, Platoon Medic Doc Johnson, and Interpreter Ali Bakar follow. Platoon Sergeant Sanders follows Jones on the right flank.

Evans has Specialist Orsman, the trained drone operator from the 3rd squad, deploy one of the platoon's Black Hornet drones to scout ahead of the platoon's movement. Orsman's job is to keep the drone aloft and at least 500 meters ahead of the platoon.

"LT, I did a full 360 sweep out 1000 meters, and there isn't anyone or anything in the area."

"Orsman, let me know when you need to switch out drones. We will take a break then."

"Roger, LT."

The paratroopers begin moving toward their designated recon area. After moving for an hour, Orsman calls,

"LT, time to switch out drones."

Evans calls the squad leaders on the radio.

"Take fifteen minutes, 50% security, and hydrate. Let me know if you see or hear anything."

Evans knows it would be easy to follow the raised railroad bed northwest toward Samawah, but it is also an easy ambush site, even with the drone scouting every possible ambush site. Instead, they strike due west for three kilometers and then turn north toward Samawah. The terrain is almost empty of vegetation, and the undulating terrain requires careful observation while moving. Although Evans and Sanders have checked and rechecked the platoon's communication gear, Evans is reassured when Orsman sends up his second drone and reports the absence of any activity along their route.

Evans has Specialist Burton, his RTO (radio telephone operator), report to the company command post that they have reached checkpoint Alpha. As he checks his map to confirm the location of and route to checkpoint Bravo, he notices a dark line across the western horizon.

Evans and Sanders know from experience that this indicates a sandstorm is in the making. Orsman makes one last survey ahead of the platoon and brings his Black Hornet drone in to secure it with the other two.

Suddenly, the wind from the west grows intense, and a fierce sandstorm extends from the west to the north. Lieutenant Evans recognizes the sandstorm is larger than usual and radios the squad leaders.

"Hunker down until the sandstorm moves on."

As the blowing sand engulfs the platoon, Evans senses it is far different than any sandstorm he has previously experienced in Iraq. The cloud is black, and the sand swirls instead of blowing from one direction. Strange streaks of light, some white, some red, emanate from the swirling sand. The sand is also blinding, and even with his goggles on, Evans can't see anything around him. He cannot imagine how a sandstorm this intense could have suddenly appeared.

What seems like hours but only lasts less than ten minutes, the sandstorm and its strange lights subside and then disappear. Evans checks with each squad and receives confirmation that while all are sand-covered and spitting out sand, each soldier is OK.

Evans attempts to confirm his location with GPS and finds no signal in his receiver. A look at the map and his aerial photography sheets from the S2 shop is disconcerting because there are subtle changes to the landscape that do not correspond exactly to the map or the photography. While confused but not yet worried, he directs the platoon to continue the mission. Further attempts to connect with the GPS satellite system continue to return the "no signal" indication.

Specialist Burton, Evans' RTO, gives the platoon leader more bad news.

"Lieutenant, I have lost all contact with the company and battalion. I have tried multiple different frequencies. It's like there is nothing but static on the air. Nobody answers our callsign. I can't understand this because I had solid comms before the sandstorm."

"Burton, keep trying. If you don't have any contact in fifteen minutes, let me know."

After moving north for another four kilometers, SGT White, the point squad leader, calls back on the platoon radio.

"1-6, we hear gunfire ahead at least three kilometers."

"Roger, 1-1, I am moving in your direction."

Evans, RTO Burton, and Interpreter Ali move up about a kilometer to SGT White. They attempt to determine the direction of the gunfire from White's description, but it ended before they joined White.

Meanwhile, Sergeant Sanders has deployed the rest of the platoon in a defensive perimeter. Lieutenant Evans returns and gives his squad leaders a quick briefing.

"Although the distant firing has ceased, SGT White is conducting a three-man recon of the area ahead. Osmond, get up to the 1st squad and keep the drone up and ahead of SGT White's recon."

SGT White heads north with two squad members, while nothing more is heard in the direction of Samawah. Orsman, after joining the 1st squad, keeps the drone ahead of the three-man patrol and warns SGT White of what is ahead until he loses line of sight with the drone. The drone automatically returns to Orsman's docking station.

It is now 1230; SGT White and his recon team have been gone for almost 30 minutes, and there are no reports of enemy activity. As Lieutenant Evans begins to plan a move north to find and support the recon team, SGT White and his two riflemen walk back into the hasty defensive perimeter. SGT White starts his report by saying,

"Lieutenant, I don't think you are going to believe me, but the train station is in great shape, and I believe there are Brits in defensive positions around it. I was able to see the station from about 500 meters away."

"Come on, SGT White," scoffs Lieutenant Evans.

"That train station was abandoned decades ago, and no train tracks exist. And I know no Brits are in our AO."

"Well, Lieutenant, I don't know how to put this, but that station looks like it was just built, and there are train rails north and south and east and west from the station. I'm not sure about the Brits because the uniforms look really old-fashioned, more like something you would see in old movies. I was able to hear some of them talking, and what seemed like the Brit accents were clear."

"Orsman, how close can you get to the train station from where we are now?"

"Lieutenant, my line of sight with the drone isn't good for more than a mile. I have to be within a mile of the station."

"Tim, did you see any bad guys?"

"Since we approached from the station's south, the barricades around the station look oriented more toward the west and the north. I saw some movement in that direction, but can't confirm who or what they were."

"Sergeant Sanders, take the second and third squads on the left, and I will take the first and weapons squads on the right. SGT Baker, once we are within a kilometer of the train station, position the machine guns and sharpshooters to cover us as we move on to the train station."

After moving two kilometers and approaching within a mile of the station, Evans has Specialist Orsman position the drone to monitor the train station. Evans is surprised that the picture on Orsman's pad clearly shows the train station complete and surrounded by barriers of stone, railroad ties, and sand mounds. His curiosity increases as the drone shows khaki-clad figures inside the train station. Most surprising is the flag that flies above the train station from a pole attached to the station's north side. Evans recognizes the distinctive Union Jack when the wind blows the flag.

It is now about 1330 and the height of the daytime temperature. The platoon moves slowly forward, with the point man of each forward squad using the undulating sand hummocks for cover as they move toward the train station. Quickly, the weapons platoon has the two M60 machine guns in position, and three sharpshooters are positioned in overwatch locations. Lieutenant Evans takes a long look at the train station from about 500 meters. The five-foot-high barriers of railroad ties, rocks, and piled-up sand surrounding the station obscure the figures in the station. Little does he know their sudden appearance is a source of consternation for those in the train station.

To those in the station, the strange flying thing that circled the station like a bird of prey provides a sense of impending dread. While each British soldier is fully resolved to do his duty, in the back of their minds, there is a kernel of fear as to what the outcome of these strange visitors will be. Although no one attempts to shoot the thing out of the sky, its sudden departure relieves a bit of the tension.

The next thing they see is a strange group of human figures dressed in some form of uniform, carrying what appears to be weapons, fanning out south of the station. Who are they? What are they? Is this some Arab trick? The soldiers at the station dare not let them get too close.

The soldiers at the station are instructed to maintain their positions and only fire if they are fired upon by this strange group. All in the station watch carefully as three strangely dressed individuals walk toward the station.

LT Evans approaches the train station with interpreter Ali and his radio telephone operator, Specialist Burton. Evans told Burton and Ali to keep their weapons shouldered. When the three step out of their covered position 150 meters from the station, they are watched closely by more than a dozen figures manning the barriers surrounding the train station. The figures behind the barricades are wary of an Arab trick and train their weapons on the three, ready to fire at the first sign of any hostile moves.

When LT Evans is about 100 meters from the station, he stops and shouts, "Hello there. We are Americans on patrol and want to know what is happening. May I speak with the officer in charge?" Interpreter Ali then repeats his statement in Arabic.

Within minutes, a uniformed individual steps from behind the southernmost barrier and approaches. As he comes near, Lieutenant Evans is surprised to see a middle-aged man with a close-cropped full beard dressed in a tan khaki tunic, matching short pants, wearing a pith helmet with khaki wrappings around his ankles and calves above hobnail boots. His tunic has two breast pockets and patches just above the breast pockets. He is carrying what looks like a Lee-Enfield rifle and has three gold strips on his left arm. He stops and shouts,

"Who in bloody hell are you, and what are you doing skulking around my railway station?"

Taken aback, Lieutenant Evans responds somewhat defensively,

"I am Lieutenant Gregory Evans, the officer in charge of the unit you have seen."

Reluctant to provide any more information if the man was some intelligence operative, Evans asks,

"When did the train station get rebuilt, and just what are you doing here?"

"Leftenant, this station has always been as you see it now. Are you American?"

"I am American, and we are members of the United States Army stationed here for the past eleven months. We are on a routine patrol around Samawah. Who are you?"

The man draws himself to his full five-foot-eight-inch frame and responds,

"I am color sergeant Paddy Beacon, Royal Welsh Fusiliers, and we are responsible for the security of this railway station. Some local rebels attempted to convince us to leave our post just a bit ago. Our lads' well-placed shots convinced them we intend to stay put."

LT Evans responds, "I didn't know the British Army was operating in this area. Do you know who you are defending the station against? We heard the gunfire when we were four kilometers away."

"Leftenant, the British Army is scattered all over Mesopotamia, and we are just one outpost given responsibility for this rail station.

The railroad still operates, and we hope to be able to take a train back to Baghdad soon. The rebels want the railroad as badly as we do, so they haven't destroyed it. But they have to have the station to control the track switches."

"Sergeant Beacon, I don't understand. We were told the station was destroyed, and the railway tracks were taken up long ago. I have seen pictures of the station in ruins."

"Leftenant, this station has remained as you see it now since it was built five years ago in 1915."

"Wait a damn minute, Sergeant Beacon. You said it was built in 1915, and it is now 1920. That can't be. It is 2022, not a hundred and two years ago."

"Leftenant, you must have been in the sun too long because we arrived here in April 1920, and it is now August 1920. If you still doubt me, I have a telephone in the station, and you can call your headquarters to confirm what I have told you."

"Thank you, but I will contact my headquarters on the radio to clear this up. Burton, when did you last contact the company CP?"

"Sir, we still haven't had commo with anyone since the sandstorm. I have tried all the frequencies, but get nothing but static on any of them."

"Sergeant Beacon, since I cannot contact my headquarters at the moment, is it possible for us to get out of the sun and join you at the train station?"

"Leftenant, how many men do you have, and what will you do until you contact your headquarters?"

"Right now, I still have a mission, but things are not as expected, so I need to reassess how best to accomplish our mission. May the 38 of us join your detachment inside the station?"

"Leftenant, you may join us at the station. I have twenty-five of the best Fusiliers in his majesty's army. But we cannot spare any water, food, or ammunition as we have been under siege for more than two days from the rebels."

"I appreciate that, Sergeant Beacon. We have our own supplies and will try not to burden your unit."

Chapter Three: Introductions All Around

Lieutenant Evans calls Platoon Sergeant Sanders to bring up 2nd and 3rd Squads while he returns and brings up Weapons and 1st Squads in front of the train station. As Evans returns with his platoon, Sergeant Beacon expresses surprise when he sees the weapons and equipment carried by the Americans.

As the Americans enter the train station, the British soldiers at the barricades show their relief when they recognize that the soldiers are not the rebels. The British soldiers watch as each American soldier enters the train station and moves to the south side.

SGT Beacon turns to LT Evans,

"Bloody hell, Leftenant. Who are you chaps, and what kind of weapons are those? I saw American soldiers during the last war, but none of them looked like you bunch."

"Sergeant Beacon, when did you last see American soldiers?"

"It was right after a bloody patch in Belleau Woods in 1917. But you lot are carrying much more kit than those lads."

"Sergeant Beacon, we need to have a long talk once we get everyone to the train station."

"Sergeant Sanders, assemble the platoon at the far end of the train station while I talk with the NCO in charge here. For a while, let's keep to ourselves."

Out of Time in the Desert

As the US soldiers drop down on the south side of the train station, the British soldiers occupying the barriers watch them with growing curiosity. LT Evans overhears one of the British soldiers' comments,

"What's with all the bits and bobs on those chaps' uniforms?"

He acknowledges the contrast between the paratroopers' full "battle rattle" and the British soldiers' khaki uniforms and pith helmets, all of whom carry the same rifle as Sergeant Beacon. Evans thinks this will take some explaining, as the size differences between the British soldiers and the paratroopers are also apparent. It is even more so when Specialist Jack Bowman, all six feet six inches, passes by a much shorter Brit. He also notices what appears to be a machine gun mounted midway along the barriers on the station's east side. The American soldiers are a little dazed and find it hard to understand where they are and who the soldiers are defending the train station. They have more questions than answers.

While SGT Sanders arranges the platoon at the far end of the station, LT Evans and Sergeant Beacon move into a small office that might have been a ticket office when the train station was operating.

The conversation opens with LT Evans asking, "What month and year did you say this was?"

"Leftenant, it's the eighth month of the year 1920."

Evans sighs, "With all due respect, Sergeant Beacon, that cannot be. We left our Forward Operating Base today, August 20, 2022. We could not have gone back more than 100 years!"

"That may be, Leftenant, but here is a copy of my orders from my commanding officer dated August 1, 1920. You will note they have been countersigned by the Commissioner for the British Mandate, Mr. Arnold Wilson. We are one of two garrisons around the city of Samawah. The other is to the north of the city and is led by Captain Highsmith."

"Do you have any contact with Captain Highsmith?"

"Only when the rebels stop cutting our telephone lines. We have not had contact with the other garrison for a day."

"Well, Sergeant Beacon, I need much more information. Can you give me some idea of what is happening and who the fighters are attempting to take this station?"

"Leftenant, I am told that it all began in the north of what the locals now call Iraq. Some Ayatollahs believed the British Mandate meant that the country would be incorporated into the British Empire. The rebellion started heavily in May of this year. We know that the tribes war with each other all the time, but now we have seen Shia and Sunni tribes work together in the uprising. I have no doubt the tribes that are attacking us are local and have been stirred up by the local ayatollah. The problem is they outnumber us, and they are well-armed. Have you not heard of the British Mandate for Mesopotamia and Palestine?"

"I may have, but that history is longer in the past than I remember. Now, I need to meet with my sergeants and figure out what we will do next."

Beacon watches Evans talk into a wire around his mouth and thinks to himself,

"Who are these Americans? I have met some Americans, but these soldiers are far different than any I have met. Their weapons and equipment are strange, and they seem to be talking to each other in a language I don't understand. The soldiers are all large young men carrying a great deal of kit. I must be satisfied that any reinforcement is good, even if we don't know who or where it came from."

As Lieutenant Evans moves toward his assembled platoon, one of the British soldiers on the barriers shouts, "Here they come." Evans calls to his platoon, "Grab your weapons and follow me. Beacon, where can we help the most?"

"Leftenant, put your men on the south and east side in case they try to come around behind us."

Evans instructs each squad leader to take a sector on the south and east, allowing the British soldiers to move to the west barricades to reinforce that sector. With more British rifles responding to the small attacking force, the attackers fall back, dragging their few wounded with them. So far, no American has engaged any attacker, and LT Evans wonders how long that will be. He turns to the radiotelephone operator and asks,

"Do we have comms with anyone, Burton?

"No, sir, we haven't talked to anyone since earlier this morning."

Lieutenant Greg Evans realizes he has a dilemma. His rules of engagement allow him to return fire if fired upon. Since they are now inside with the British forces, they have been fired upon. He doesn't know what his unit can or cannot do to support the British. Since he has no communication with anyone in his chain of command, he must rely on his assessment of the situation. Or, as one of his instructors at the Infantry School said, "In some cases, it might be better to seek forgiveness than permission."

With that in mind, he assembles his squad leaders and platoon sergeant and attempts to explain what is happening and what their mission has become.

"So, troops, it should be obvious now that things are not what we expected. I don't know how we got here, and I don't know how we will get back. I have learned that the Brits defending this train station are part of a British force in Iraq, or what they call Mesopotamia, and the year is 1920. As best I can tell, we have somehow traveled back 102 years. I looked at the overhead imagery of the train station before we left the FOB, and it was demolished. I can't explain why it is in good shape now or why we are with a group of British soldiers who look like they just walked out of World War I. I have been told that there is a large group of folks out there who want to take this station and will kill all those defending it. Our arrival here has now more than doubled the number of soldiers at the station."

He continues, "I believe how we survive to return to our time and families depends on how well we can help the Brits defend this station. Our mission is now to join the force defending the station. Once that is completed, we can figure out how to return to our time and place. If we fail here, we may never return, and no one will know what happened to us. So, let's gear up and be prepared to be a part of the defense. Any questions? SGT Jones?"

"What the hell, sir? How can we get back, even if we help the Brits?"

"I don't know the answer. I do know that if we die here with the Brits, we will never get back. So, let's do what we can to stay alive and help the Brits. I will meet with Sergeant Beacon, the Brit NCO in charge, and see how we can beef up their defensive plan."

"Sergeant Sanders and squad leaders, we must conserve food, water, and ammunition. We have no idea how long this will last."

LT Evans asks the medic, Doc Johnson, to check if any medical personnel are with the Brits.

Quickly determining there are none, Doc Johnson reports that the water supply is in pretty bad shape, and none of our guys should drink from it without filtering it or using the water purification tablets. He also requests permission to use the old baggage office for his aid station and will prepare to treat everyone as necessary.

LT Evans and Sergeant Beacon spend the next hour revising the station's defensive plan. The station is oriented roughly north and south, fifty feet long and 30 feet wide. The train tracks run along the east/northeast side of the station, and riflemen are positioned behind barricades on all sides of the building, using whatever is available to put in front of them.

LT Evans suggests that rather than keep British soldiers in one area and American soldiers in another, they can maximize their effectiveness by integrating the forces. Sergeant Beacon says most attacks come from the north and west. LT Evans says he can have two machine guns providing overlapping fire if one is on the north corner and the other on the west corner. He tells Beacon that he can put three snipers on the roof to reach out almost a thousand yards and possibly neutralize some rebel leaders during the

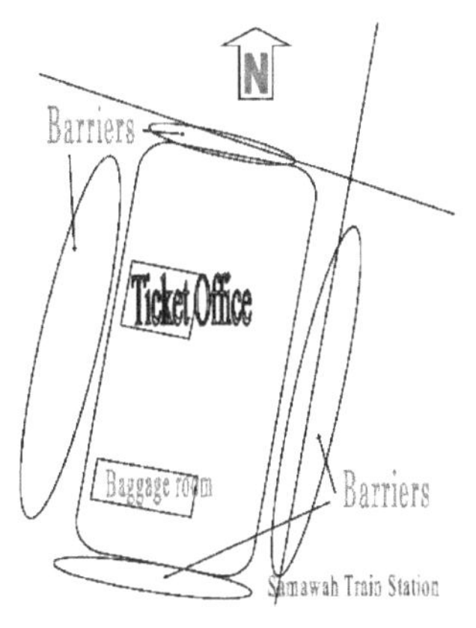

attacks. Beacon expresses his surprise at the various weapons Evans' soldiers carry and makes a note to himself to learn more about them.

Beacon is enthusiastic about the plan and calls for Corporals Bramble, Ledger, and Lodge to incorporate the Americans into the defense. Evans introduces his rifle squad leaders, Sergeants White, Davis, and Jones. He tells Beacon that the squads operate as a team, and while they will work with his troops, they are a team and know best how to operate together. He introduces SGT Baker, the weapons squad leader, and tells Beacon he will organize a reaction force that can move to any threatened part of the station.

Beacon then has his three corporals, each assigned a squad of Americans, introduce them to their soldiers and take their place in the defensive perimeter. As night falls, the British and American soldiers get to know each other and explain how their weapons and equipment are used.

The Brits are amazed by the light weight of the M4s, while the Americans can't believe the weight of the Lee-Enfields. The British soldiers are increasingly curious about the equipment carried by the paratroopers and have some difficulty understanding the use of water purification tablets, night vision devices, and the vests used by the paratroopers equipped with grenade launchers.

Corporal Bramble and SGT White move to their soldiers. SGT White introduces Corporal Bramble and his squad to the four privates Bramble has with him. White has to listen hard because he can tell Bramble is speaking English, but his accent is so strange he catches only half of Bramble's introductions.

To the side, Corporal Bramble asks,

"SGT White, what is all that kit you carry? It seems your lads are covered with equipment I've never seen."

White is disconcerted because he has no way to answer the question. After all, how do you explain 21st-century equipment to a 19th-century soldier? Bramble notices White's discomfort, changes the subject quickly, and asks.

"SGT White, where are you from in America?"

"Chicago." draws the quizzical response from Bramble,

"Where is that in America?"

Bemused, White replies,

"In the Midwest."

"I am from the midlands, but me family is mostly Welsh. The majority of the company are Welshmen. We are the Royal Welsh Regiment. As you can see from our cap badge." He pulls off his pith helmet and shows White the cap badge of the Royal Fusiliers.

"Corporal Bramble, how long have you been in the Army?"

"Nigh on fourteen years. Me father was in the regiment, so I followed him." 

"How long have you been here in Iraq?

"You mean Mesopotamia? The regiment has been here since we left France in 1919. We thought we might return to England for some refitting and recruiting, but the blokes in Whitehall said that we were better off here.

"And you, SGT White, how long have you been in service and this godforsaken country?"

"Eight years in the US Army, and we have been deployed for almost eleven months. I hope to get home in less than thirty days. I can't wait to get on that airplane for the flight home."

"How is that? Are you going to fly in an aircraft from here to Chicago? That's not possible."

"Corporal, believe me, things have greatly changed since your time and mine. We will fly from here to our station in North Carolina, where our division is based."

Meanwhile, SGT Davis, Corporal Ledger, SGT Jones, and Corporal Lodge introduce their soldiers. Shortly after they have made their way around the barricades, Jones and Lodge return inside the station, where Lodge says,

"Bloody Hell, SGT Jones, is soldier Oldham a woman?"

"She is, Lodge, and a damn good soldier. She can outshoot and outmarch most of the men in the platoon. She has proven herself many times over the past two years. She is also an ace with her grenade launcher. I believe you will find out soon enough how good she is."

"Things may get sticky, SGT Jones. My lads haven't seen an English or any woman in over a year."

"I understand, Lodge, but Oldham can take care of herself. Should anyone try anything with her, they might soon learn she is quite good at hand-to-hand combat."

"I hope she never has to demonstrate those skills. The rebels are a nasty bunch when it comes to women."

Out of Time in the Desert

As the day draws to a close, Evans suggests to Beacon that some night reconnaissance activities could help. They might learn how many they face and possibly disrupt the attackers' planning. Beacon expresses some concern about operating at night but assumes LT Evans has something else to show him.

Chapter Four: Night Recon and First Attack

The decision to conduct night operations was a simple one for Evans. He had no intelligence on the rebels and their dispositions in the area, so some sort of recon was imperative. Once he finds Sergeant Beacon, he tells him he will mount a night reconnaissance mission.

"Leftenant, that is not wise. We have no idea how close the rebels are, and you will likely stumble upon them in the dark. Losing men in the dark is a certain disaster."

"Sergeant Beacon, we have some things we haven't shown you."

"SGT Sanders, have Orsman bring up one of our Black Hornet drones and a second set of NODS."

Orsman hands the drone to LT Evans, who turns to Beacon and says, "Paddy, this is our eye in the sky. It can go out a mile and take pictures for us. It also has the nighttime capability to see the body heat signatures of fighters and where they are. See this little screen that Specialist Orsman is holding? That is the screen that shows us the pictures taken by this little bird."

"My God," exclaims Beacon. "How is this possible? I now believe that you've come from the future. We have never had anything close to this in any army I know of."

LT Evans then flips down the NODS attached to his helmet and tells Beacon, "One more thing: These give me the ability to see at night. It's not magic, just advanced technology that magnifies the available light so I see in the dark."

Beacon sits back down in the only chair in the ticket office and says, "Leftenant, how do I tell anyone what we have seen? These are abilities my soldiers dream about."

"Sergeant Beacon, let us worry about that when the time comes. Right now, we have many more pressing problems with the rebels."

At 0130, LT Evans and SGT Davis, 2nd squad leader, and two riflemen, Richert and Johnson, put on camouflage paint, mount their night vision headgear, and do a final internal radio check before leaving the blacked-out train station. Sergeant Beacon and LT Evans had established a challenge and password earlier, and the four-person team slipped out of the station ten minutes later and headed northwest.

Evans thought about having Orsman use the Black Hornet drone's thermal capability to cover their movement, but realized the twenty-five-minute loiter time for the drone wasn't enough. Orsman did a complete perimeter sweep with the drone before the recon team left and verified no one was within a mile.

There was no moon, and the night was very dark. While the night observation devices (NODs) provided good coverage, the team moved slowly to avoid unwanted contact. After moving more than six kilometers northwest, the team spotted the glow of fire about three kilometers away due north. Moving slowly forward until they were within a kilometer of the fire, all four swept the area around them for sentries. Using his daylight binoculars, Evans could see several men around the blaze, but no sentries or anyone appearing to be a guard. He could see over fifty Bedouin-style tents filling the valley as they looked around the area. Evans estimated that each tent had at least ten fighters and realized they faced a rebel army of nearly 500. Evans had each team member surveil the camp before giving the signal to return to the station.

The four quickly moved west for two kilometers and then headed southeast toward the railroad station. They found no more encampments and did not encounter anyone. Orsman again reassured LT Evans that no one was within a mile of them. Once close enough to be challenged, the four members gave the password and entered the station.

LT Evans called Sergeant Sanders and Sergeant Beacon over.

"I have some bad and some good news. We estimate about 500 rebels, a little more than four miles from here. We couldn't tell how they were armed, but saw no artillery or mortars. Paddy, if you haven't received any artillery or mortar fire, I assume they have none."

"Aye, Leftenant, we haven't received any artillery fire, but I don't see much good news. The rebels still have many more guns than we do. We also don't have much hope of resupply or reinforcement."

"In that case, we must maximize what we have. Can you give me the number of weapons you have and how much ammunition for each weapon? I will detail what we have, and between those numbers, we can figure out how best to defend this station. Since we saw no sign that the rebels were going to attack tonight, let's get some rest and review what we have come first light."

"Aye, says Beacon. Our lads are on half alert so they can have some rest."

"Lieutenant, I recommend we send out two patrols at first light to see if any rebels have moved closer to the station. With Orsman scanning ahead of the patrols, we should have plenty of warning."

"I agree, Sergeant Sanders. Sergeant Beacon. Could you have two of your corporals accompany the patrols?

"Leftenant, as long as your eye in the sky is there, my lads will be quite happy to join your patrols."

"SGT Jones, have 3rd squad take the first light patrol to the south and east and have Orsman use the drone to scout out in front."

"I'll take Corporal Lodge with 3rd squad." Replies Jones.

"SGT Davis, have 2nd squad take the second first light patrol to the west and north. Orsman will scout for both of you."

"Roger, sir. I'll have Corporal Ledger with us."

At first light, the two patrols depart the station. LT Evans and Platoon Sergeant Sanders begin their weapons, ammunition, and supplies inventory while heating their coffee. Sanders starts by confirming that the platoon of 38 has 33 M4 carbines with 300 5.56mm rounds each. The M60 machine gunners each have 1000

7.62mm rounds. The three light machine guns, M249, have about 700 5.56mm rounds. The M110 sniper rifle marksmen are carrying 200 7.62mm rounds. The three squads with M320 grenade launchers have sixty rounds between them. Sanders said he was surprised to learn that a half dozen soldiers were carrying two M67 fragmentation grenades each.

LT Evans and Sergeant Sanders then meet with Sergeant Beacon to learn that his 25 soldiers have 25 rifles with less than 50 rounds left for each. They also have two Vickers light machine guns with approximately 500 rounds between them. Evans asks if any range markings have been done around the station. Beacon doesn't understand his question and asks,

"What in the bloody hell do I need range markings for?"

"Our weapons work best when they are used at their optimal ranges. For example, our marksmen can take out an enemy soldier at a thousand yards, and knowing the distance makes them much more lethal. The heavy machine guns are best used against area targets between 600 and 800 yards. The light machine guns are best at 200 to 300 yards."

"I see," says Beacon. "I'll have one of the lads step off the distances and put a stake in the sand to make the yardage. Say, 100, 200, and 400 yards?"

"Sergeant Beacon, that would be most helpful to my soldiers."

"Leftenant, what are those things in your ear and alongside your mouth?"

"These are part of the platoon radios that each squad leader, the platoon Sergeant, and I use to communicate."

Beacon, slightly confused, asks,

"What are they, and how do they work?"

A little exasperated, Evans replies,

"Sergeant Beacon, it would take too long to explain how radio technology has evolved over the last hundred years, but just believe me, Sergeant Sanders, the four squad leaders, and I communicate using these. All paratroopers now have these radios."

Looking even more confused, Beacon asks,

"Leftenant, what do you mean by paratroopers? Are you some sort of cavalry? I've never heard of paratrooper cavalry. Is this something the American army organized?"

Evans is tired and replies,

"Paddy, it is too long a story for tonight. How about I explain it all later?"

"That's fine with me, Leftenant. I just can't work out what paratrooper means."

As Evans and Beacon walk the perimeter to place the various weapons, the patrol that went out earlier to the north and east runs back into the station. Corporal Ledger, the Brit with 2nd squad, catching his breath, tells Beacon and Evans,

"We saw at least a hundred rebels heading this way from the north. It looked like they were dragging a heavy machine gun on a gun carriage. Wil Williams has just finished putting the stakes in on the north and west."

"SGT Sanders, two marksmen to the roof with one grenadier. As soon as they see any sign of a heavy weapon, their first mission is to take out the operators and, if possible, the weapon."

Specialists Orvis and Blackman, the designated marksmen, and Specialist Backus, with his M320 grenade launcher, hustle up the ladder to the train station's roof. Soon, prone behind hasty barriers of wood, the three prepare to take on the attackers.

LT Evans looks around the station's perimeter and sees that his squad leaders have fully integrated their riflemen into the established defensive positions of the Brits. The M60 gunners are behind barriers on the north and west sides of the station, with good fields of fire for any approaches from the north. The M249 light machine guns remain with the squad leaders, prepared to reinforce any sector of the defensive perimeter. He and Beacon look at each other and realize that all they can do now is wait.

While they wait, Beacon looks at Evans and quietly asks, "Is one of your soldiers a woman?" Evans chuckles to himself and responds, "Yes, Specialist Oldham is a female. We have a number of them in our units. I guess you can say that things have changed a lot in a hundred years."

Beacon shakes his head and mutters,

"Bloody hell, now I must worry about a woman."

Evans laughs and says, "Don't you worry about her. She is as good a rifleman as any in the unit and tougher than many."

Specialist Blackman calls down from the roof,

"I have a large group about 2000 meters due north. They don't have any crew-served weapons that I can see."

The other marksman, Specialist Orvis, calls, "I have a large group due west about 2500 meters away, moving this way and dragging what looks like a heavy machine gun on a wheeled cart."

"Blackman and Orvis, you fire only after the rebels have fired on you."

That restriction immediately becomes moot as rifle rounds begin falling around the station, obviously fired from a great distance. The American squad leaders and British corporals remind their soldiers that they should only fire on confirmed targets and waste no ammunition on hidden firing positions.

Orvis and Blackman simultaneously call,

"Engaging targets, 1000 meters west, northwest." As rifle fire on the station increases, American and British riflemen behind the barricades hold their fire, waiting for enemy targets to appear in range.

Out of Time in the Desert

The steady crack of the two sniper rifles punctuates the rattling of random bullets hitting the walls and roof of the train station.

Blackman calls, "I have a heavy machinegun setting up at 1000 meters north, northeast, am engaging crew."

LT Evans cannot see the enemy machine gun and assumes Blackman is suppressing its crew.

When he looks around the corner of the barricade, twenty fighters in brown and black robes crest a sand hill 300 meters to the north and fire on the station. 1st squad's automatic weapon quickly downs half of the group, and the other half quickly retreats. Sergeant Beacon appears at Evans's side and says,

"That's what the rebels do. They try to find a weak spot in our defense. Your boys made mincemeat out of that attempt."

Within minutes, a much larger group of approximately thirty appears on the west side and fires a volley of rifle fire at the station. As they advance, the two M60 machine guns fire sharp three-round bursts from each corner, and the rebels are caught in a deadly crossfire. Less than ten manage to escape to the east.

Evans recognizes that the assault groups are staging behind sand hills 500 meters north. He tells the squad grenadiers with the M320s to put two 40mm rounds each behind the sand hills. Although just beyond the effective range of the grenade launchers, all four rounds land around the sandhill, and those on the roof see robed figures fleeing north.

Blackman calls down from the roof,

"We took out the machine gun crew with 40 mike mike, but I'm not sure if we damaged the weapon."

The silence that follows is eerie, as only the sharpshooters, machine guns, and grenadiers have fired their weapons. American and British riflemen look at each other and silently recognize that this first test was too easy.

LT Evans, Sergeant Beacon, and Platoon Sergeant Sanders meet in the old ticket office and review this latest action.

Doc Johnson checks on the three soldiers nicked by flying splinters from the station walls. He walks quickly to the two noncommissioned officers and reports,

"SGT Sanders and SGT Beacon, the injuries are minor and didn't need more than some disinfectant and Band-Aids. We are good to go."

Sergeant Beacon watches Doc Johnson return to the makeshift aid station and remarks to Sanders,

"You have a bloody doctor in your outfit?"

"We do," says Sanders, "and he can do most anything in the field to care for the soldiers."

Beacon heads into the station ticket office, scratching his head.

"I think that was a probe to see what we have in the station," says Evans as they gather in the ticket office.

"Aye, we had only seen one or two small groups assault us before you came, and they were very cautious and disorganized. We had no difficulty convincing them to leave us be."

Sanders says, "They appeared pretty organized this time with separate attacks from two directions. Is it possible they have new leadership?"

"If they do, we should expect more coordinated attacks," says Evans.

"We need some quick reinforcement ability where the enemy hits us hard. I recommend we take a squad automatic weapon from 1st squad and three riflemen for a reserve," says Sanders.

Evans calls Tim White, the 1st squad leader,

"Have 1st squad prepared to be a reserve force to move anywhere in the station. SGT Sanderss will brief you shortly on who will be part of the reserve."

Sergeant Beacon looks at Evans and says, "Now I see how your radio thing works. You talk into it, and the others hear you in their ears."

"Pretty close." Says Evans.

LT Evans asks SGT Sanders to walk with him around the station's perimeter. As they walk, Evans turns to Sanders,

"Jeff, how are the troops handling this? Do they really understand that we are a hundred years in the past?"

"Lieutenant, I'm not sure what they really understand. But we need to take some time to visit each squad and remind them of our situation."

"You're right," says Evans, "but other than outlining what happened and where we are, I can't tell them much more than what we all know. Certainly, the first and most important question on their mind is how do we get back, and I can't even begin to answer that question."

"Maybe, Lieutenant, the best answer is to win this fight first, then we can figure out how to get back to our base and finally to our families."

"Right again. Let's meet with each squad, and you and I can use that approach."

Evans and Sanders spend the next three hours visiting squad after squad. As expected, every soldier wants to know when and how they will get back. As Specialist Backus so eloquently puts it,

"This place is a shithole, and now we are a hundred years back in shit? It can't get much worse than this."

Encouragingly, each soldier acknowledges that they must fight their way through this before they can get back, and they owe some loyalty to the poorly equipped British soldiers who have been left to defend the train station.

Out of Time in the Desert

The British soldiers cannot help but overhear the remarks of some of the paratroopers. Private Mack Jones, one of Beacon's assistant gunners, turns to Specialist Richert from the 2nd squad and asks,

"Bob, where are you fellas from? I know a little about America, but you all seem to be from nowhere in particular. Everyone in our regiment is from Wales, even though some are from Ireland, but they say they are Welsh."

Richert, now on a first-name basis with the closest Brits, replies:

"Mack, that is why we are called the 'All Americans' because we represent all of the fifty states of the United States."

"I see you wear a double A on your sleeve, and it's for All American. But what is that word above the double A? I have never seen that before. Airborne?"

Richert is now wondering how he will explain to someone in the 19th century how airborne soldiers in the 21st century jump from high-performance aircraft to land and fight. Lamely, he responds,

"Mack, it is the type of infantry unit we are. Airborne is just the way to get to the battlefield and fight. In thirty-five years, you will see many more of our type."

As the afternoon heats up, Evans and Sanders head back to the ticket office, which has nominally become the command post. Before they enter, Evans quietly remarks to Sanders,

"The battalion S2 told me that the town of Samawah and this train station were the site of one of the bigger battles of the 1920 Iraqi rebellion against the British. Let's keep it to ourselves that the rebels wiped out the Brits defending the train station."

"Thanks, Lieutenant. I did not want to hear that, but maybe we can change history if we successfully defend the station."

As they greet SGT Beacon, LT Evans tells the two,

"We must go on the offense against the rebels. During our night recon last night, we got close to their camp. What if we could get within four hundred meters and lobbed some grenades at the camp? That might shake them up."

Beacon quickly responds, "Leftenant, I agree, but my lads don't work well in the dark. Can you go out again in the dark?"

Sanders quickly adds, "I can lead the three grenadiers and two riflemen out tonight after midnight and introduce them to modern weapons."

"Jeff, don't take any unnecessary chances. We need you all back here and not stuck in some dune."

"Never fear, Lieutenant, I want to return to my family just as much as anyone here."

Chapter Five: Offensive Night Action

At midnight, Sergeant Sanders and Specialists Oldham, Backus, Richert, PFC Smith, and PFC Jones prepare for their night patrol. Sanders reminds the three with the M320 grenade launchers that they will be using them only if they can get within 400 meters of the rebels' camp. Oldham replies,

"Sergeant, I can drop an egg on the bad guys from 500 meters. Why do we need to get closer?"

"Robin, I know you are good with that, but I want us to be able to hit them hard. We must be closer to identify possible leaders, supplies, and equipment that can be hit. It won't make as big a splash if the rounds land in some sand pit. Oldham, Backus, and Richert, what's your load of grenades?"

The three say they each have ten high explosive (HE) rounds and three flare rounds.

"Let's gear up and move out. Richert, you were on last night's recon. Can you take the point? We don't want to go out like you did, so take us a different way."

With a shrug and an "OK, Sarge." Richert prepares to lead the team into the darkness.

The night vision devices show a ghostly landscape as Richert heads west of the station. Orsman's drone scours the area for human heat signatures and radios Sanders,

Out of Time in the Desert

"You are all clear for the next mile."

Listening for any sounds and sweeping the terrain ahead, left and right, the six move about four kilometers west and then turn north. Richert stops and whispers in Sanders' ear,

"If we come in from the west, they won't expect anyone from that direction."

The four move for another thirty minutes and notice the glow of a fire in the distance. As they move toward the glow, they scan the terrain, looking for sentries or outposts. They move toward a small hill that overlooks the area where the light of a large fire originates. The large fire interferes with Sanders' night vision, and he has to switch to his regular binoculars. He notices about a dozen robed individuals gathered in a tent facing the fire. About ten meters behind the tent is a stack of what can only be ammunition boxes. Bedouin-style tents stretch haphazardly across the rest of the shallow valley.

Sanders motions for the six to move back below the crest. He pulls the three with grenade launchers close and whispers,

"I think the leadership is having some meeting close to the fire. There appears to be an ammunition storage just behind them. Multiple tents are scattered all around the area. Here is what we are going to do."

"Richert and Oldham, I want you to put two HE rounds in the group gathered in that tent facing the fire. Your aim point should be just the other side of the fire. Backus, I want two HE rounds on the stack of ammo about twenty meters behind the group facing the fire. All three of you then fire an illumination round and then follow with two HE rounds on the tents. Take your time on the first two rounds, but get the illumination and final HE rounds out as soon as possible. I will give you the word to begin firing. Now flip up your NODs because the fire provides enough light. As soon as you complete firing, drop 20-30 meters, put your NODs back on, and wait for me to signal that you can move out. Everybody got that?

Now, Smith and Jones, you have to secure our rear. If you see anyone behind us, come up and tap me before we have the grenade launchers do their thing."

Affirmative head nods are all the answers Sanders needs. Silently, the three grenadiers arrange their grenade rounds on their carrying vests so they can quickly fire and reload. Each now has an HE round in the chamber and slowly inches back up to the crest of the small hill. The scene is just as Sanders described. Each grenadier lines up their sights for maximum elevation and looks toward Sanders. Sanders picks up his binoculars and whispers,

"Fire."

Three M320 grenade launchers cough in unison, and Sanders can almost see the projectiles arch into the air as the three grenade launchers again cough out one more HE round. Sanders blinks as the first rounds bracket the tent where the robed figures sit. The explosion shatters the night, and the tent and the twelve figures are blown in two directions, their robes torn and shredded. There is no doubt that the grenades were effective. An accompanying explosion in the ammunition storage area punctuates the night. Suddenly, the night is lit by three bright flares drifting down over the many tents. As robed figures emerge from the tents, forty-millimeter grenades explode all around them. In less than two minutes, the three grenadiers have launched twelve high-explosive grenades on the unsuspecting rebel camp. Sanders watches the pandemonium that ensues. He realizes that they have probably accomplished much more than they had hoped.

Quickly, the four slide back below the crest of the hill, don their night vision headgear, and join Smith and Jones. The six lay quietly and look for any movement in their direction. Seeing none, Sanders gives Richert the move-out signal, and the spread-out six silently head back toward the train station. Slowly moving west, the six continue to scan the area for any signs of movement in their direction. Again, the undulating plain ahead is still, while small explosions punctuate the silence behind them. Orsman, who has kept the drone circling a mile out, tells Sanders he is clear once he sees them approach.

Within fifty meters of the train station, Sanders answers the challenge with the new password, and the six cross the barriers and drop down on the station floor.

LT Evans and SGT Beacon join the six, and before they can ask how the patrol went, Oldham excitedly says,

"Lieutenant, you wouldn't believe it! Those sonsabitches were blown all to hell! Richert and I put two rounds into their robes from 400 meters, and they are now little pieces."

Backus adds, "I think we blew up their ammunition dump because after I put two rounds in the stack of boxes that continued to cook off long after we left the area."

Sergeant Sanders completes the results,

"Lieutenant, when the illumination rounds went overhead, people popped out of the tents just in time to get hit with six rounds of HE. I don't know how many we killed, but there is a shit load of fighters that we won't have to worry about today or tomorrow."

"Congratulations all around. You have made it much more difficult for the rebels to take the station. Get some rest. Take it easy on the water and chow. What you have is all we will have for a while."

As the still-hyped soldiers return to their squads, LT Evans turns to Sergeant Sanders and SGT Beacon.

"Jeff and Paddy, we didn't expect to be out more than 12 hours. We must figure out how to get food and water for the troops. Let's get some rest and, at first light, see what we can work out."

As Evans and Sanders walk back toward their part of the station, Sanders turns and asks,

"So, you call him Paddy? I know we dropped some formality and used first names among the NCOs, but is that his first name?"

"Jeff, I'm not sure what his first name is, but he introduced himself as Paddy, and his soldiers call him that."

"Lieutenant, even if he weren't a hundred years older than me, he would still be old enough to be your grandfather. Can you imagine a soldier who survived the trenches of WWI and is stuck in this shit-hole fighting off Iraqi rebels? Some of these Brits haven't been home in years. I have a lot of admiration for Beacon and his soldiers."

"The issue of a hundred years forces the question, have you figured out how we will return to our time?"

"Jeff, I haven't had much time to work on that. I know it's weighing on the troops, and I hope we can keep them focused on the situation. Once that is resolved, we may figure out how to get back. I know that sounds lame," says Evans, "but it's the best I have right now. Once the morning patrol is ready to go out, we will get with Paddy on the food and water."

The morning starts slowly with groans and complaints about no coffee from the Americans and no tea from the Brits. An overcast sky mirrors the mood of the soldiers manning barriers as the morning patrols head out.

Evans and Sanders review with Paddy Beacon the raid results that night, and his questions begin with,

"What did you say you shot the rebels with? How does it explode on them from that distance?" Sanders tries to explain the workings of the M320 grenade launcher and the high-explosive rounds they fire. He calls SGT White and asks him to bring up an M4 with a M320. Paddy Beacon marvels at the M4 and M320 as SGT White explains the operations of each weapon and loads an HE round. He comments, "If only we had these in the big war, things would have been different."

"It still takes a trained soldier, regardless of what weapons he may have. What was it like in France during the war, Sergeant Beacon?" asks SGT White.

"Lad, the two years I was in France were the coldest and the wettest they had ever had. I don't remember being anything but cold and wet all the time. Most of my mates were sick half the time. It was either the influenza or trench foot. For the second year, we lost more to sickness than to the Germans. When the shooting stopped in '18, less than half the regiment was able to stand to."

Evans now brings up the most pressing issue: food and water. "Paddy, is there any way for us to get food and water?"

"We were told there is a well about a mile or more south, and some of my lads said they saw sheep near there. It might be useful for us to send out a water party that might also find some mutton."

"That might be our only hope, Paddy. My maps don't show any water for many miles, and all of it is north with the rebels. Sergeant Sanders and the group that went out need rest. We can work out how to get some water and food later this morning.

Chapter Six: The First Big Attack

As Evans, Beacon, and Sanders meet to work out how a water party might be organized, the joint patrol of SGT Davis's 2nd squad and two riflemen from the British regiment come running into the station. SGT Davis says,

"Lieutenant, we saw two columns of ragheads headed this way. One approaching from the north and the other from the northwest. I estimate at least 200 in each column."

"Did you see any crew-served or heavy weapons?"

"No, sir, I did see what looked like a light machine gun, but I can't be sure."

LT Evans then looks at Sergeant Beacon and says, "Looks like we stirred up the hornet's nest last night. Let's get the troops ready for an attack."

"Aye, Leftenant. Four hundred rebels will test us for sure. But overall, we are better off now than a day ago."

Sergeant Breshear, the British second-in-command, and Platoon Sergeant Sanders start at the east and south of the barriers and remind the soldiers to engage only when they have a clear shot. Most soldiers, both American and British, know they have only the ammunition they are carrying, and attacks may go on for days. As Breshear and Sanders meet near the north side of the barrier, they see the dust from one of the columns in the distance.

Out of Time in the Desert

Within minutes, the first long-range rifle fire lands around the barriers. The well-disciplined American and British soldiers hold their fire. The first group of twenty attackers sprint toward the station's north side while some intermittent rifle fire from the west provides covering support.

As the first attackers reach the 300-meter markers the patrols have set out, the M249 light machine guns fire three-round bursts into the twenty. Half the twenty fall from the fire, while others continue firing wildly as they advance. Single shots from M4s and Lee-Enfields punctuate the three-round bursts of the M249s. No attacker reaches within 75 yards of the barriers on the station's north side.

As the defenders are about to take a breath, a larger group of 40-50 rebels moves on the station from the west. They, too, are disorganized and often fire wildly as they move. At 400 meters, the M60 machine guns begin a hail of interlocking fires, and almost twenty of the rebels fall. Their bodies now slow those following, and another ten suffer the same fate. Small groups of five to ten in the northeast try to surround the station on the north, east, and south. The M320 grenade launchers and M249s target each group. As each small group falters or falls wounded, the cries of the wounded add an eerie postmark to the slaughter. Individual American and British riflemen quickly take out running and retreating rebels with single, well-aimed shots.

LT Evans, SGT Sanders, and Sergeant Beacon move quickly along the line of the barricades and tell the soldiers to stop firing.

"Hold fire, hold fire," yells Evans.

The cries of wounded rebels break the silence as slight, hajib-wearing figures are seen moving toward the fallen and ministering to the wounded.

"That's their women," says Beacon in amazement.

The American and British soldiers are stoic, imagining who will be there for them if they are wounded. Soon, men dressed only in loincloths move to each group of bodies. The wounded are put on makeshift litters and moved from the field of carnage. It takes more than an hour for the wounded to be removed. The dead remain in the open. Evans wonders how long they will be there before the stench is too overpowering.

Soon, four small carts, each pulled by the same one or two men in loin clothes, approach the groups of dead rebels. They load as many as eight bodies on each cart one by one and carry them off beyond the rise 3000 meters away.

As Evans checks his watch, he realizes that it's only 1030. He calls Sanders for a personnel check. Sanders reports on the radio,

"All accounted for and no wounded."

All this bloodletting has lasted less than ten minutes, and the removal of the dead and wounded more than forty.

Beacon returns shortly after making his rounds with his corporals and joins Evans, shaking his head.

"Leftenant, none of my lads were touched by the rebels. Your weapons do much more damage than the rebels were expecting. Do you think they are returning, or have they given up?"

"That depends on how badly they need the station," replies Evans.

"Why do you have to hold the station, and why do you think they want it?"

"The railroad is our only way of moving men and supplies," Beacon explains.

"If we lose this station, our garrisons north and south will be completely isolated. The rebels need the station for the same reason. The switches at the station control the tracks running north, south, and east-west."

Evans looks over the carnage they have exacted on the rebels and says,

"I think the rebels are not going to mount another attack today. I suspect that we have taken out some of their leaders, and they need more than a few hours to regroup. We need to work on food and water for our soldiers. We may be here for many more days."

As he finishes his assessment of the attack, the last cartloads of bodies are seen making their way north, punctuating his view that the rebels will take some time to regroup.

At 1200, Beacons offers to have his soldiers, who have scouted to the south and identified a well, lead a joint patrol for water and food. SGT Sanders has his squad leaders gather all the platoon's empty canteens and empty two-liter water bladders. SGT Baker is designated as the patrol leader. British Privates Chalker and Johns and Specialists Backus and Johnson join him, each carrying a load of empty canteens. Interpreter Ali joins the patrol to provide his support if they meet any locals and need to bargain with them.

Chalker and Johns look at the plastic US Army canteens carried by Backus, Johnson, and Baker as they leave.

"What make canteens would those be, Backus?" Says Chalker in his broad Welsh accent. Even though he is not entirely sure he understood Chalker, Backus acknowledges the finger Chalker points to the plastic canteens and water bladders.

"It's the plastic type issued to all of us. These two-liter water bladders fit on our gear, and the long straw allows us to drink without taking out a canteen," replies Backus.

"Did your boys have those in the Great War?"

"I think not," says Backus. "Their canteens were much more like the ones you carry, metal with a cover."

"Aye," says Chalker. "Too much metal and not enough water."

Chapter Seven: Water and Food

When the water party gathers outside the barricades, SGT Baker asks British Private Chalker to guide them south toward the suspected well. At 1330, Privates Johns and Chalker and Specialists Backus and Johnson, each carrying a load of empty canteens and water bladders, slowly move south in a spread formation. Interpreter Ali and Specialist Orsman bring up the rear with their share of empty canteens just behind SGT Baker.

After a day in the sun, Specialist Orsman has his drones fully charged from the foldable solar panels. The tiny drone ranges ahead of the patrol, moving silently back and forth. He calls SGT Baker every two minutes and reports no movement on their route. The patrol continues for almost four miles when Orsman taps Baker and says,

"There is a small group of buildings about a half mile ahead, around what looks like a well. The bad news is that I see about four men with weapons sitting outside one of the buildings. The good news is I also see three or four sheep in a pen alongside the building."

SGT Baker halts the patrol and gathers the group to relay the latest information. Upon hearing Baker's report, Private Johns says,

"Eh now, SGT Baker, how do ye know what's ahead of us? We haven't even seen anything."

Baker points to the now loitering and barely visible drone about fifty feet in front and fifty feet above them and says,

Out of Time in the Desert

"Johns, this is our eye in the sky, and Specialist Orsman here can see what's ahead and tells me over our radio."

Johns shakes his head in disbelief and exclaims,

"Do you Yanks have some sort of magic that can make things fly and tell you what is ahead?'

"Nothing like that, Johns. It is the technology that we have in our time. It might be hard to believe, but you will have the same thing in about 100 years," says Baker. "Now, let us figure out how to deal with the four armed men and how we might get water and food."

"Ali, do you think you can talk with them? We have some Iraqi money, but I believe paper money won't get us much even if they recognize it."

"SGT Baker, let us see if we have anything we can use for barter. If they are poor goat herders, it might be possible to trade for water and a goat or two."

The next ten minutes are spent looking through their packs, web gear, and pockets for anything they might be used to barter. Backus and Johnson offer shaving gear, razors, a small mirror, and small cakes of soap. Johns and Chalker offer their mess kits, each with a small oblong tin, a knife, a spoon, and a fork. No one looks happy as they volunteer their items.

"SGT Baker, I will try to contact them without showing myself and see what the response may be. If they are friendly, you and I can carry the barter items. I will do my best to persuade the men to take these in turn for water and two goats. Once we agree, the rest can bring up the water containers."

Ali leads the patrol toward a small mound within fifty yards of the dwellings. He then calls out in Farsi to the four men sitting in front of the largest building. They immediately jump to their feet and look toward the sound of his voice. Soon, there is a back-and-forth between Ali and the four men. The oldest of the four is the leader or Elder, whose voice quickly silences the other three.

After six exchanges between the Elder and Ali, Ali turns to SGT Baker,

"They are not part of the rebels. They are more aligned with the British than the groups further north. They say they are willing to share their well. I believe negotiating for two of their animals may be difficult."

"Ali, how about their weapons? Should we be prepared to fight them?

"SGT Baker, I think not. Their weapons are old and mostly for show. I suggest we shoulder our weapons and proceed like allies."

Ali tells the Elder how many they have in their party and that filling their water carriers is a priority. Slowly, Ali and SGT Baker enter the small group of buildings and head to the well. Just as slowly, three women, one older and two younger, arrive at the well and start drawing water. The other four soldiers approach slowly, laden with the canteens, and place their loads around the well. As each bucket is lifted by the older woman and emptied into the dozens of canteens and water bladders, Ali continues to discuss their need for food with the Elder.

"SGT Baker, can you join me with the barter items?

Baker lays out the shaving gear and soap on a blanket one of the women provided.

"They have little need for shaving but are very interested in the knife you carry on your belt, SGT Baker."

"That is a very expensive knife, and I hate to give it up. A longtime friend made it, especially for me. Can we get two goats for it?"

"I think with the mess kits from Chalker and Johns, it might make the deal work. The women like the bright patches you wear on your uniforms and would gladly trade some flour for them."

Baker, Backus, and Johnson peel off their full-color American flags and the red, white, and blue 82nd Airborne shoulder sleeve insignia from their shirts and lay them on the blanket.

In short order, the six now heavily laden soldiers begin their hike back to the train station. Each soldier carries more than ten canteens of water and one or two two-liter water bladders. Three also have one-pound bags of flour. The two British soldiers lead two plump goats on five-foot ropes.

The five-mile hike back to the train station takes almost three hours. Six exhausted soldiers are greeted with cheers by those at the station.

Platoon medic Johnson directs that the water in each canteen be treated with a water purification tablet before drinking. SGT Baker confesses that he had to drink some water along the way. Recognizing that he may have had contaminated water, Baker heads to his squad area, exhausted and now very worried.

Sergeant Beacon calls for Private Ned Jacks and introduces him to the US soldiers.

"Ned is our butcher and cook. He can make any piece of meat taste like the roast your Mammy made. Let him butcher the goats and cook the meat over the fire for dinner."

SGT Evans finds Baker. "Corey, you did well. We expected some water. The meat is going to make everyone better off. And the flour is a real bonus. You accomplished your mission and more."

"We couldn't have done it without Ali. He figured out who the folks were and how to get us the water and food we needed. He should get all the credit. I hope the water I drank doesn't come back to haunt me."

"Jeff, I worry about my wife. I haven't heard from her in a couple of weeks. I just missed a chance to do a FaceTime call before we went out."

"Corey, I'll make sure LT Evans knows Ali's part. I'm glad you came through for us. Make sure you let Doc Johnson know if you start to feel any bad effects from the water. After all the shots we got and eleven months in country, you will probably be OK. As soon as we get back to the FOB, I'll try and get you a call to your wife as soon as possible."

As Sanders leaves Baker's squad area, he notices that Brit private Ned Jacks is quickly butchering the goats and will soon have them ready for the spit he had constructed earlier.

Sanders finds Paddy Beacon and asks if they can talk. Outside the barriers on the south side of the station, Sanders asks Beacon, "Paddy, when you leave here, where will you go?"

Beacon is slow to respond and finally says,

"Sergeant Sanders, I donna know. Our other closest outpost is inside the city wall of Samawah. We could reinforce them, I guess. But who knows what the Colonels and the Generals are thinking now? I have learned that those of us on the ground go where we are told and do what we are told to do."

Sanders chuckles, "Paddy, things haven't changed in a hundred years. We still have the same situation. To change the subject, what will you tell your senior officers about our joining you in this little station?"

Out of Time in the Desert

"Aye, Sanders, you have the same problem. What will you tell your American leaders about our little brouhaha here in Mesopotamia?"

"Paddy, it beats the hell out of me! But I think your problem is a little bigger because you have seen technology unavailable for almost a hundred years. How can you explain that?"

"Sergeant Sanders, I think your problem is far greater than mine. I am in a time and place I have always been. You, my friend, must return to your time and place."

Soon, the smell of roasted meat begins to fill the train station. British and US soldiers who have been on reduced rations for days find their mouths watering, anticipating something more than canned or packaged food.

Sanders finds the other three squad leaders and tells them everyone will be on 50% alert. Half can go and eat while the other half stand watch. Each squad leader will decide who goes first. Sanders then tells SGT White, "If you make Booth wait to eat, the poor guy might never forgive you. I have seen how Specialist Booth eats, even when he says he isn't hungry." White says, "Never fear, Platoon Sergeant. Specialist Booth is lining up for chow as we speak. I guess one goat will be enough for him. What is everyone else going to eat?"

Later, after a quick and fulfilling piece of the mutton served by Private Jacks, Sanders finds LT Evans, and they enter the ticket office together.

Out of Time in the Desert

As they enter, Beacon says, "The telephone line must have been repaired. I have just been told an armored train will pick us up tomorrow on the north and south tracks."

"When will that be?" says Sanders.

"I canna confirm when, but battalion headquarters is adamant that we are to leave the station on the train tomorrow."

"That sounds like good news, Paddy. On what track will the train arrive, and in which direction will you be going?"

"If I am correct, the train will come from the south, and we will go north to the detachment in Samawah."

Chapter Eight: Another Night on the Town

LT Evans and Sergeant Sanders look at each other with the same question: "What do we do when the Brits' train comes?" They both realize they have less than 18 hours before deciding: stay and see if they can return to their time or go with the Brits and take their chances outside the current combat zone.

Evans is the first to give his view, "I think we must stay here. We somehow ended up here, and the chances of returning from somewhere else don't seem as probable."

Sanders agrees immediately and adds, "What if some of the troops think going with the Brits gives them a better chance?"

"I don't think that's possible, Jeff, but we need to talk with all the troops and outline why we must stay here, even if it is hard. Meanwhile, we must take advantage of the night and give the rebels another taste of airborne firepower. They may attack us during the day, but we own the night."

At dusk, the soldiers in the station enjoy roast mutton and biscuits fried in the fat of the goats. Using some of the seasoning he has squirreled away, Private Jacks has made the mutton tender and tasty. By dark, little is left on the bones, and British soldiers enjoy their tea while American soldiers savor a cup of coffee for the first time in two days.

Evans and Beacon discuss the options for a night attack on the rebels.

"I think we can pull off something like we did last night, Paddy. The rebels will certainly be wary, and we can expect to run into some sentries around their camp."

Beacon agrees, "If I were the rebel leader, I would want my lads to spread out and not be the concentrated target they were last night. So, you may encounter more than one group tonight."

"I wonder how a much larger force might inflict even more damage on the rebels. We could put a force of twenty of our soldiers in their camps in the middle of the night and force them to reconsider any attacks the next day. If we have enough night observation devices that still work, it could make future attacks difficult for them,"

"I think you are on the right track. Leftenant," says Beacon. "The rebels don't fight at night, so leaving the station as it was when you arrived for a couple of hours tonight should not be a problem."

Evans turns to Sanders, "Jeff, have the squad leaders round up as many working NODs as possible, and let's see how large a force we can put together for tonight.

Thirty minutes later, SGT Sanders returns and tells LT Evans, "Sir, we only have fourteen working NODs even after scrounging all the batteries from everyone in the platoon. Too many in the platoon didn't bring their solar recharging units for their NODs."

"Fourteen will have to do, Jeff. Now, how should we configure our little task force? We want the M320 grenadiers and the M249 machine guns. With me, Ali, and Burton, that makes nine; who else?"

Out of Time in the Desert

"Lieutenant, we can put the platoon radios on three team leaders, and you will be able to communicate with each team. Leaving Burton here will lessen your load, and if we can communicate with anyone, Burton will be better off here than out there with you."

"Jeff, I agree. Now let's form up the three teams. With a grenadier and a machine gunner in each team, can we afford to have a squad leader in each team?"

"No, sir. I need two squad leaders here. I suggest you have SGT Davis lead your first team, Specialist Walker from the 3rd squad, and Specialist Booth from the 1st squad be the other team leaders."

"Jeff, good suggestions. I will fall in with Walker's team when the need arises. Pick two riflemen for each team, and I think we have the task force formed."

At 0100, on the third day, the fourteen-member assault team gathers inside the train station. LT Evans looks at SGT Davis, Specialist Walker, and Specialist Booth and does a quick radio check—three answers of "five by" tell him they are ready. Davis is joined by PFC Johnson with an M320 grenade launcher, Specialist Foreman, and Specialist Orsman and his drone console. Carrying his machine gun, Walker is joined by PFC Blake with an M320. PFC Janes and PFC Johnson. Also taking his machine gun, Booth is joined by Specialist Oldham, PFC Shocky, and PFC Cross.

Orsman launches his first Black Hornet drone and scouts out a mile for any sign of fighters. Finding none, he says,

Out of Time in the Desert

"LT Evans, the route is clear for at least a mile.

LT Evans calls SGT Davis, "Ron, start due west for two miles, and let's see what we find. Walker, you cover the right flank 20 meters from Davis' last man. Booth, you are on the left and 20 meters from Davis' last man.

Every soldier staying behind in the train station douses any lights or flame, leaving the station in total darkness. SGT Davis leads the assault team out of the barricades and heads due west. The night is moonless, and the night vision on each soldier's helmet paints the terrain in stark shades of black and grey. Orsman asks for a halt for him to scan the area ahead. He quickly reports a small group of approximately twelve individuals more than half a mile ahead. The group appears to be both men and women. He recommends they move due north and avoid the group. Davis turns north, and the group follows.

Orsman's drone continues to scout ahead of the assault group. More than a mile away, two fires appear on the horizon—one fire on the west and one on the east, about 1000 meters apart. Orsman shows LT Evans what the drone is monitoring. The screen shows two groups about the same size, possibly thirty to forty. There is no evidence of any women.

There is some high ground almost in between the two groups, and Evans begins to develop a plan of attack. Getting the assault group together, Evans explains his plan to hit both groups simultaneously.

Out of Time in the Desert

"We will set up on the high ground. SGT Davis will attack the group to the west, and I will lead the attack to the group to the east. Davis will have Johnson, Orsman, and Foreman. Booth will have Oldham, Cross, and Shocky. Davis will have two M320 grenade launchers and one machine gun. Booth will have one M320 grenade launcher and one machine gun. Orsman will continue to monitor the drone until we reach the line of attack."

Evans shows each soldier the pad with the high ground circled as their attack launch site and indicates the line of attack for each team. The distance from the high ground to each group is roughly 400 meters.

"On my command, each grenadier will launch two 40mm high-explosive rounds directly into their respective groups. As soon as the grenadiers fire, the machine gunners will lay down a base of fire on the group. The grenadiers will fire an illumination round, allowing each rifleman to fire on individual targets as they present themselves."

"I want the machine gunners to fire only one box of linked 5.56 and each rifleman to fire no more than two magazines. Once you have fired on each group, move to the rally point. I will mark it with a chemical light that you can see with your NODs."

"Any questions?"

Each of the thirteen nods affirmatively and hoists their weapons.

Orsman has just launched his second drone, sweeping the area between the two groups and the route to the high ground.

"LT, no one is along the route, and the two groups appear to have bedded down."

As Davis leads the team to the high ground, they separate into the two assault elements, with Davis' team facing west and Booth's team facing east. The grenadiers prepare and load their high-explosive rounds and put the illumination rounds on their ready vests. The two machine gunners line up their weapons, snap in a fifty-round box, and rest their bipods on the rocky ground. Evans now checks the status of each group of rebels and asks Davis and Booth if they are ready. Davis and Booth both send a quick, "Roger, ready." Evans gives a quiet command, "Fire."

The three grenade launchers cough in unison once and then twice. Before the first round explodes in the two groups, the grenade launchers again cough in unison, and parachute flares open above each group of rebels. Machine gun fire quickly begins, knocking down anyone standing.

There is now concentrated rifle fire on both groups. Four riflemen and a machine gunner in Davis' group and three riflemen and a machine gunner with Booth are hitting targets at will. Each group of rebels is now in chaos. Each time one of them sits or stands to fire, they are knocked down by the US weapons. Any rifle fire in response to the paratrooper's attack is wild and ineffective.

The paratroopers finish firing nearly simultaneously as the parachute flares die on the ground. Each paratrooper drops their NODs and heads to the rally point in the dark. Reaching the rally point, Evans asks for a headcount. As he says each paratrooper's name, he quickly receives thirteen excited, "Here, sir."

Evans smiles to himself and says to the team, "Well done, troopers. I think we hit them as hard as we could. Orsman, keep scanning to see any other rebels in the area."

"All clear, LT."

"SGT Davis, lead us back to the train station."

While they are moving south, they enjoy the exchange of fire between the two groups they just attacked.

Booth laughs and whispers, "Those ragheads have started shooting at each other. They must think each attacked the other. They may finish what we started."

"LT, " says Orsman, " The group we saw enroute to the attack site is still active. I recommend we move west around them. The route back to the train station is clear after that."

After another two-mile slog, the fourteen enter the barricades in a single file. Sergeant Beacon and Platoon Sergeant Sanders are there to greet them. "Any casualties, Lieutenant?" asks Sanders.

"I think Blake may have sat on a scorpion. To his credit, he screamed pretty quietly."

Blake, hearing the Lieutenant's comment, responds, "Lieutenant, I was sure I was shot in the ass, but that was before any shooting."

Smiling, Evans says, "I can't recommend a Purple Heart for a scorpion sting. But you'd better have Doc Johnson look at it. An infection now could be a big problem."

"No sweat, sir. I am on my way to see Doc."

Beacon and Sanders, almost in unison, turn to Evans and ask, "What happened?"

Evans, now feeling the after-effects of the adrenaline high of the attack, yawns and says,

"We hit two camps. We set up in between the two and hit them with grenades, machine guns, and rifle fire. It was so quick and so violent that the rebels didn't respond until we were well away from them. As we left, they began firing at each other, thinking that the other camp was attacking them. If one group was Sunni and the other Shia, we might have helped split the larger group into the two religious factions."

Beacon shakes his head and says, "Leftenant, you have done more damage to the rebels in the past two days than I think they ever imagined. Your ability to fight at night takes away their larger numbers and will give them pause. After the fight yesterday and tonight, I wonder if they still have the stomach for a fight."

"I hope you are right, Paddy. I want nothing more than to see you and your men off on the train tomorrow without having to fight anywhere along the line. Meanwhile, I need to grab some sleep. Tomorrow may be an important day for all of us."

Out of Time in the Desert

As Evans and Sanders head to where they are bedding down, each has the same question on his mind. What do we do when the Brits leave?

Chapter Nine: Day of Reckoning

As the morning patrols, now integrated British and American soldiers, converge, the surrounding area is eerily silent. LT Evans, Platoon Sergeant Sanders, and Color Sergeant Beacon settle on the benches of the train station's ticket office as the first lights of dawn brighten the barricades surrounding the station.

"Paddy, do you know when the train will be coming for you and your men?"

"Leftenant, all that was heard before the line was again cut was that an armored train would be coming from the south. We were to board and expect to reinforce the lads in Samawah. Will you and your soldiers be joining us?"

"Paddy, we haven't decided yet. SGT Sanders and I are still figuring out what we must do to return to our unit. There are still too many unknowns."

"Aye, I understand. When we rejoin our regiment, how do I explain what you have done to support our defense of the station? Will anyone believe me?"

"I see your problem, Paddy. I believe ours is just as big. Can we convince anyone that we were here in 1902 fighting alongside a unit of the British Army?" replies Evans.

Since first light, Specialist Orsman has had his drone moving out a mile or more north and west. As he flies the drone to the north, he sees armed, black-robed individuals diligently lifting the rails from their ties and stacking them off the rail bed. He finds LT Evans and quickly shows him what is on his pad.

LT Evans calls SGT Beacon over to his side of the ticket office and shows him the work of the rebels to disable the train rails.

"Well, that's a hell of a mess," says Beacon. "It's much easier to take the rails apart than to put them back together, but without those rails, a train will go no further than the station. I don't think that was what our regimental commander expected."

"SGT Sanders," says Evans, "Can we get an assault team out there quickly to discourage any more rail damage?"

"We can. I have alerted SGT Davis to take his squad and follow the rails north and take out any ragheads working on the rails. Orsman will monitor their movement and cover their flanks."

SGT Davis quickly organizes his squad and puts Specialist Booth's M249 light machine gun on point. He instructs the squad sharpshooter, PFC Skip Orvis, to be prepared to overwatch as they approach the rebels.

Quickly moving along the raised railroad bed, SGT Davis and the 2nd squad are monitored by Specialist Orsman and his drone. Orsman calls Davis,

"Ron, you have seven ragheads about a half mile away. I don't see any others within a mile of them, so it's not an ambush site."

Davis tells his squad members to double time along the tracks. Once Orsman tells him the rebels are just 500 meters away in a cut through the small hill and around the corner, Davis has Orvis move off the tracks and find an overwatch site. Once Davis sees Orvis in the prone position above the hill, he spreads the remaining squad members in a line. The five quickly advance on the rebels around the corner and drop all seven. Now, Davis looks over the tracks and reports back to LT Evans.

"One Alpha, the rebels have removed two railroad tracks. They look undamaged, but none of my guys know how to put them back correctly."

LT Evans turns to SGT Beacon and asks, "Paddy, do you have anyone with experience replacing rails?"

"I think we may. Young Mack Jones once worked on the rails in France. Let's see what he can do."

SGT Brashear, Beacon's second in command, brings in Private Jones. Beacon asks Jones, "Mack, do you know how to replace train rails?"

"Aye" says Jones, "but I need a good rail sledge and the proper amount of spikes. Without those, it's a nigh impossible job."

"Lad, this is a train station. Surely, you can find the tools to mend the rails somewhere here. Let's get the boys looking. Leaving by train is not happening without those rails repaired."

LT Evans calls SGT Davis and instructs him to set up around the dismantled rails and await a repair team. Orsman continues to send his drone north and west. No rebels are seen within a mile north or west.

Davis places his squad in a rough circle around the small hill and awaits the repair team.

Private Jones calls SGT Beacon to say that they have found a sledgehammer and some rail spikes. Beacon orders Brashear to take two riflemen and Jones to SGT Davis as quickly as possible.

As Brasher and his three soldiers reach Davis and his squad, Orsman calls Davis. "Ron, you have two ragheads a mile west of you. They are headed your way. They are carrying weapons."

"I have them in sight," says Davis. "Orvis, when you have a clear shot, take out the two before they can get any closer."

As Orvis watches the two rebels approach, Jones, Breasher, and two soldiers move the rails back onto the raised rail bed and begin spiking them down. As they finish, two shots from Orvis' sniper rifle cut through the air, and he reports to Davis, "Two down." Davis calls Orsman for the status of the west and north.

Orsman replies, "Nothing moving west or north. You are clear."

As Davis moves to the repaired rails, Corporal Brashear slaps Jones on the back, "Well done, lad. We may have you make corporal one day."

Davis calls Evans, "One Alpha, we are all secure and repaired. I recommend 1-2 stay in place for at least a couple more hours in case more attempts are made."

"Concur," replies Evans. "We will have 1-1 relieve you at 1300."

Out of Time in the Desert

Platoon Sergeant Sanders calls SGT White, "Prepare to relieve 1-2 at 1300.

Evans, Sanders, and Beacon get together on the station's north side. Evans offers his thoughts first,

"I think the rebels are taking up the track because they think reinforcements may be coming from the north. If so, should we plan on protecting the rail line until the armored train arrives?"

"How can that be done?" replies Beacon. "The next garrison north near Samawah is over five miles from here. It took the rebels most of the night to remove that part of the rails. We may be in the clear if there are no more sabotaged rails before nightfall."

"I think we need to be more aggressive with the rail protection," says Sanders. "If Orsman and his drone could recon another few miles north, he could almost reach within two miles of the garrison around Samawah. A small recon team could do it."

Evans agrees, "Paddy, how about a mixed team of your soldiers and ours watching over the rails? Our soldiers could be your eyes and watch out over a mile away. Yours would provide the firepower to counter any small group of rebels making for the rail line. I'll ask SGT Jones to take that mission with his squad and Orsman, the drone operator. "

"Leftenant, that sounds jolly good."

Sanders calls SGT Jones to the ticket office. Evans outlines what he thinks needs to be done. "Trent, we need to have a small team along each mile of track. Orsman will stay with you and continue to monitor your movement north."

Evans turns to SGT Beacon. "Paddy, I think five or so of your best riflemen would add to the effectiveness of the mission. When the train comes from the south and picks up your main body here, the soldiers along the track can be picked up as you move north. Our paratroopers will then return and join us here in the station."

"That sounds like the best plan, Leftenant. But what will you and your lads do once we are gone? Could the rebels see we have left and then come after you?

"While that is possible, we must focus on getting the train here and moving north with you and your soldiers. We will work out what to do after that."

To himself, Evans thinks, I haven't a clue what we will do after the Brits are out of here. Sanders and I need to think carefully about our next moves.

Evans radios SGT Davis and SGT White, updating them on the new plan. He directs that as soon as the combined patrol of SGT Jones's squad and the Brits arrives, Davis and White return to the train station. White's 1st squad, now only halfway to relieve Davis and the 2nd Squad, turns around and heads back to the station.

SGT Beacon has now organized his team of soldiers led by Corporal Breasher. Breasher introduces the six riflemen to SGT Jones and his squad. Having spent the last 48 hours together, most have had the opportunity to meet each other more than once. Senior Privates Johns and Bigham look at Specialist Oldham.

Johns says, "Oldham, are you as good with the wee rifle as you are with the big shotgun?"

"Johns," says Oldham, "If I can see it, I can hit it. Unfortunately for you, I can see a bit further than you. " She points to the scope mounted above her M4.

Johns, slightly annoyed by the Oldham's response, tells Backus to lead the team to the train tracks and north.

As they pass White's 1st squad, the 1st squad members look quizzically at the combined team of nine paratroopers and five British soldiers. The contrast in uniforms and weapons is striking.

Thirty minutes later, Jones finds Davis and asks how he has deployed his squad. Davis explains, "I have the marksman on the hilltop and the machine gun in a covered position, ready to move."

Davis recalls his squad and asks PFC Johnson to lead the squad back to the train station. Specialist Orsman has continued to monitor the areas north and west. The drone returns to the docking station when its battery reaches 10%. Orsman launches his second drone and sets up the solar charger for the returned drone.

"SGT Jones, I need to remind you that each drone has about thirty minutes in the air before it returns, and the range is about one to one and a half miles."

"No problem, Orsman. We will always be within your scan area."

Jones has Specialist Walker set up his machine gun just below the rise and the designated marksman Bozeman on the top of the rise, where he has more than a mile of visibility north and west. He assigned PFC Curcio to be Walker's assistant gunner and British Privates Williams and Stith to Walker's post. Jones now moves down the railroad elevated bed and asks Orsman if there is any other high ground within a half mile. Orsman identifies a small rock outcropping on the west side of the rail line and shows Jones the picture from the drone. As they move north, Jones taps Bozeman and Oldham to occupy the high ground ahead. Breasher tells Jacks and James to join Bozeman and Oldham. Jones estimates they are about three miles from the station and need only one more strong point to deter any rebel moves on the railroad.

Orsman identifies another higher elevation point a mile or more ahead that Jones believes will satisfy the need for the final strongpoint.

"Corporal Breasher, will you take the lead on this strong point with your two soldiers, Johns and Bigham, and Specialists Johnson and Blake? Both our soldiers are armed with grenade launchers.

"Aye, SGT Jones. We will move on it now."

"Orsman will stay with me, and we will have a small reinforcement team of the four of us."

As he finishes his conversation with Breasher, Orsman says, "Trent, we have a group of six moving on Bozeman's position. They are about a mile out from them and moving very carefully. They appear to be carrying some boxes that might be explosives."

"I don't have comms with Bozeman. Do you think he sees them?

"I'll have the drone point him in the right direction. When the bad guys get more in the open, Bozeman and his crew should see them."

Orsman sends the drone directly over Specialist Bozeman's head. He wiggles the drone and repeatedly flies it toward the approaching rebels. Bozeman gives the drone a thumbs-up, acknowledging he sees the approaching group. Orsman then scouts further west to see if there are other threats. Seeing none, he flies the drone to the north and again finds no threats.

Bozeman calls to the three team members, "Heads up, bad guys, at our nine o'clock. Each of you take a look with the binoculars so you can see the approaching rebels."

Oldham spots the two carrying a box and wonders if one of her 40mm HE rounds would ignite any explosives.

She turns to Bozeman, "Why don't we let them get within range of my M320, and you and the other two take out the ones not carrying the box? I can then take out the box and the two carrying it."

"Robin, how close do we want them to be? Is 400 meters about right?"

"Jack, no problem. When I shoot, you three count to three and then take out the other two. The grenade will get there when your rounds hit the other two. OK?"

The four wait and watch. Bozeman had ranged the distances and counted off the distances to the four rebels. "550, 500, 450, 400. Ready, Robin?"

"Firing," says Oldham, as her grenade launcher coughs once.

At the count of three, the other three place well-aimed shots at the two rebels alongside the two carrying a box.

Suddenly, two robed rebels stagger. A split second later, a large explosion engulfs the four rebels. As the smoke clears from where the four rebels were, Specialist Bozeman calmly says, "Guess they were carrying some sort of explosive after all."

Having never seen a grenade launcher, Private Jacks turns to Oldham and says, "Jasus girl, what did you just do to those poor bastards? Tis the most amazin thang I have ever seen. How didja do dat?"

Oldham pulls out a 40mm HE round and shows it to Jacks. "This has a kill radius of about five feet. I think I hit the box, which caused the explosion. Most of the time, all you see is a cloud of dust when this hits."

SGT Jones radios LT Evans, "1-6, the last attempt at the railroad has been taken care of. No further threats have been identified."

LT Evans radios Jones, "1-3, we have a train coming from the south. It should be at the station within the next two hours."

"Roger, 1-6, we will see how far north we can secure the rails."

Out of Time in the Desert

Jones has Orsman scout as far north as possible with the drone and turns to Brashear,

"Corporal, a train will be at the station in two hours. When the train departs the station and heads toward us, it will slow down, and you and your men are to board the train quickly."

Back at the station, Beacon and his soldiers gather their gear and prepare to board the train when it arrives. LT Evans and SGT Sanders watch with admiration as the Welsh soldiers silently and efficiently pack up their gear, shoulder their weapons, and stand by for Beacon's orders.

As the train pulls into the station, Evans and the other members of the platoon gawk at the monstrous steam engine. Surrounded by steel plates and bristling with machine guns, each car appears to have as many as twenty soldiers in each one.

The British soldiers quickly board the train. SGT Beacon strides up to LT Evans, stomps his heels together, and salutes smartly in the traditional British open-hand salute. LT Evans returns the salute and reaches for Beacon's hand to shake it in farewell. Beacon squeezes Evans' hand and says, "Leftenant, I am certain we would not have made it without you. I don't know how to tell my command how this happened, but we owe you great thanks."

Beacon realizes LT Evans has placed something in his hand while they shake hands. Opening his hand, he sees a brass coin with an engraving. Before he can respond, the train whistle blows, and an officer on the train calls out, "Get aboard, or you will be left."

Beacon boards the train and gives one last salute to the platoon of American paratroopers.

The train quickly accelerates and moves to pick up the remaining soldiers stationed along the tracks.

The train slows as it approaches the first strong point. British Privates Williams and Stith jump aboard as they wave farewell to the American paratroopers. The scene is repeated at the second strong point as Privates Jacks and James join their comrades aboard the armored train. At the last strong point, Corporal Breasher tells SGT Jones he is fortunate to have served with him. He pulls his cap badge off his pith helmet and gives it to Jones as he, Johns, and Bigham step into the slowly moving train.

Jones moves the small team quickly south along the rail line. To the west and north, Orsman keeps a close watch with the drone. Finally, after gathering his squad from the remaining two strong points, Jones leads them to the train station's barricades. The remaining squads stretch across the barricades, manning them in a 360-degree formation.

Evans calls his squad leaders together in the ticket office and says, "We have won the fight so far, as the British contingent defending this station is on its way north. I didn't share the history of this unit with you, but historically, the Brits defending this station were wiped out.

I guess we have changed history. How much so is yet to be seen because I still haven't figured out how we will return to our unit, the FOB, and time. If we retrace our steps, we may be able to find a way back. I don't think the rebels will try anything. They surely have seen the train headed north. We may expect a recon party to see if anyone is still here. If they send one, I think we can discourage them easily. I am open to suggestions."

"Lieutenant Evans, a bunch of us have chewed on this problem all the time we have been here, and we trust you and SGT Sanders will make the best decision."

"SGT White, I appreciate your confidence. I think we have had enough for today. I suggest we get with the troops and see how they handle it."

As the four squad leaders leave the ticket office, they notice that the sky has darkened and the wind has increased considerably.

LT Evans walks outside the station and sees a dark cloud on the western horizon. As he watches, it soon grows into a monster sandstorm. Moving quickly back into the station, he calls the squad leaders and tells them to tie down anything that can be blown away. Orsman tries vainly to bring in his drone, but it nose-dives into the ground.

At once, the station is engulfed in sand. Evans again sees the bright yellow and red streaks emanating from the swirling sand. As he hopes that this might be the vehicle that gets them back to their time, he sees parts of the train station falling around them. Strangely, the station pieces are almost transparent as they fall left and right; the walls are suddenly gone, and the barricades that protected them have vanished. Instead of standing on the station floor, he is now up to his ankles in debris. This all happens within the few minutes they are engulfed in the sandstorm. The sandstorm ends as quickly as it started, and Evans and his soldiers are now standing in the ruins of the train station. There is no roof and no walls. A few scattered stones indicate where the walls may have been.

Specialist Burton suddenly shouts, "I have comms! The company RTO just called me, and I answered. Lieutenant, the CO wants to talk to you, and he sounds pissed." Evans takes the handset,

"Lion six, Tiger six, over."

"Tiger six, where in the hell have you been? We haven't heard from you in more than six hours."

"Lion six, I will need to report in person. Would it be possible for our transport to meet at the previous drop-off point?"

"Tiger six, I will, but you have much explaining to do. Out."

SGT Sanders has formed up the platoon with SGT Davis's squad leading.

The platoon arrives at the pickup point, easily guided by LT Evans's now-operating GPS unit. As they are carried back to the FOB, Evans and Sanders try to think of the best way to describe where they have been and what they have done. Evans wonders if this could have been some mass delusion, but he knows that what happened was real.

"I think we just tell it like it is and hope for the best," says Sanders.

Evans replies, "I can't think of anything else to do unless we can find out what happened to Beacon's unit in 1920. "

As the platoon dismounts the armored personnel carriers, it looks nothing like the platoon that supposedly left less than eight hours ago. Filthy, unshaven, and covered in dust and sand, the squad leaders keep their squads in the barracks and only allow them to shower and eat.

Evans and Sanders slowly walk toward the company command post for a disconcerting briefing on what happened on patrol.

Chapter Ten: The Epilogue

Captain Charles starts, "OK, Lieutenant, just what the hell happened? You were out of contact for more than six hours, and your platoon looks like it's been in a hell of a firefight."

"Captain, because this will be hard to believe, I have asked Platoon Sergeant Sanders to help me tell the story because it's almost too much to tell. First, we have been gone for three days, not eight hours. Second, we spent three days with a British Army unit in 1920 defending the train station at Samawah from a large army of rebels."

"Now, that is the most outlandish story I have ever heard. How did this all happen?"

"As best we can tell, a strange sandstorm threw the platoon back a hundred and two years into the past. This same type of sandstorm brought us back to 2022 in the last two hours. Captain Charles, I can think of one way to corroborate what we experienced. If you ask Captain Bronson, the S2, to join us, I think it will help."

Captain Charles tells his RTO to contact the S2 shop and see if Captain Bronson can join them for a few minutes. Evans then asks if the CP has internet access. Captain Charles indicates it does but asks what they need it for.

Just then, Captain Bronson arrives, and LT Evans asks,

"I know this sounds strange, but could you give Captain Charles, give a rundown on the uprising in Iraq and how it affected the area around Samawah?"

"Briefly, the British were badly outnumbered in several places, particularly in Samawah. The train station in LT Evans recon area was the site of a bloody battle between the Brits and the rebels. According to the history books, the Brit detachment of the Royal Fusiliers was wiped out at the train station by the rebels."

LT Evans then asks, "Captain Bronson, will you look up the rebellion against the British on the internet?

Still puzzled, Bronson goes to a laptop and quickly types in the query for the Iraq rebellion. As he reads, he exclaims, "This can't be right. It says the British detachment at the train station decisively defeated the rebels in August 1920. Sergeant Beacon, who led the defense of the train station, was awarded the Victoria Cross for his actions over the four days of the siege. They went on to relieve the detachment outside Samawah and were one of the first regiments to return to England. Captain Charles, this is wrong. I have a printout from this same site from last week with a vastly different story of the siege of the train station."

Captain Charles turns to LT Evans and SGT Sanders and says, "OK, now you two tell me what happened."

LT Evans and SGT Sanders alternate between what happened on the first, second, third, and final day when they got the Brits on the armored train as it headed north.

SGT Sanders remembers the cap badge one of the Brits gave to SGT Jones and pulls it from his pocket.

"Captain Bronson, could you verify that this cap badge given to one of my squad leaders is from the Royal Fusiliers regiment?"

Again, Bronson uses the internet to pull up the regimental badges of the Royal Fusiliers. Looking at the badge held by SGT Sanders, he says, "This cap badge is from the early part of the 1900s and is the cap badge of the Royal Fusiliers of the British Army in Iraq in 1920."

Captain Charles shakes his head and tells Evans and Sanders, "Keep your paratroopers isolated from the rest of the battalion. I want someone from Division to come and talk with all of them. This is a story that I don't know how to handle and would just as soon have higher headquarters deal with it. You two, get a shower, get some chow, and keep away from the rest of the battalion."

As Evans and Sanders return to their platoon, Sanders says, "This should be an interesting next few days."

Evans replies, "Not sure they will be enjoyable ones."

Not surprisingly, the officers from the Division who interviewed each platoon member concluded that they had all been subjected to a shared delusion. The delusion was so strong that they believed what had happened was real. Over time, however, many of the paratroopers began to doubt whether it had happened at all. The event was never documented in any official reports, logs, or communications. The platoon returned with the rest of the Brigade and was dispersed to other battalions.

After his military commitment ended, LT Evans left the Army and became a history teacher in his hometown in southern California. His specialty was the Middle East and the early twentieth-century British Mandate for Mesopotamia and Palestine. Many students considered his history classes to be some of the best in the high school. Some students remembered how he seemed to have lived some of that history.

Although the history books do not record such events, a board of inquiry held in London in 1921 determined that the small detachment of Royal Fusiliers responsible for the security of the train station near Samawah, Mesopotamia, gallantly defended it for four days and demonstrated the utmost dedication in accomplishing their mission. Color Sergeant Michael Beacon was awarded the Victoria Cross for

his courage and leadership, and Corporal Brashear, the Military Cross for his exemplary leadership.

Beacon kept the coin he received from LT Evan and placed it alongside the Victoria Cross in his home. His children often guessed at the strange markings on the coin. Many years later, a grandson serving in the British Parachute Regiment recognized the coin as belonging to an Airborne unit of the American Army. As his grandfather had passed away many years before, he never learned how Pappy Beacon came to have the coin.

Cast of Characters

Americans

Name	Role
Greg Evans	LT Platoon Leader
Jeff Sanders	Platoon Sergeant
Tim White	1st Squad Leader
Ron Davis	2nd Squad Leader
Trent Jones	3rd Squad Leader
Corey Baker	Weapons Squad Leader
Ali Bakar	Interpreter
Skip Orvis	Sharpshooter, 1st Squad
Jim Backman	Sharpshooter, 2nd Squad
Jack Bozeman	Sharpshooter, 3rd Squad
Charley Booth	Machine Gunner, 1st Squad
Bill Catron	Machine Gunner, 2nd Squad
Chris Walker	Machine Gunner, 3rd Squad
Bill Burton	Radio Telephone Operator
Doc Johnson	Platoon Medic
Jack Johnson	Rifleman, 1st Squad
Bob Richert	Rifleman, 2nd Squad

Out of Time in the Desert

Name	Role
John Backus	Rifleman, 3rd Squad
Robin Oldham	Rifleman, 3rd Squad (only female in platoon)
Fred Orsman	Drone Operator / Rifleman

British

Name	Role
Color Sergeant Pappy Beacon	Outpost Leader
Sidney Breasher	2nd in Command
Bushey Bramble	Corporal
Tiny Ledger	Corporal
Bagger Lodge	Corporal
Bob Chalker	Senior Private
Raymond Johns	Senior Private
Bob Bigham	Senior Private
Jim Stith	Private
Tim Smith	Private
Jocko James	Private
Wil Williams	Private
Ned Jacks	Private
Victor Mayberg	Machine Gunner
Mack Jones	Assistant Machine Gunner

Weapons and Equipment

Americans

M4 carbine 5.56 mm/M17 pistol 9mm

M110 Sniper rifle, 7.62mm

M249 Light MG 5.56mm

M4 Carbine w/M320 Grenade Launcher

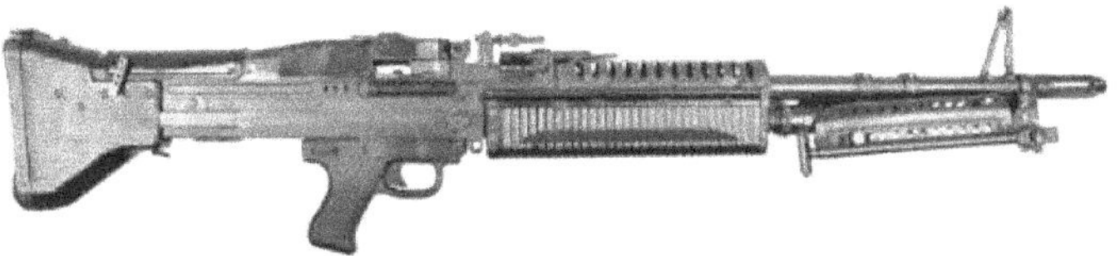

M60 Machinegun 7.62mm

British

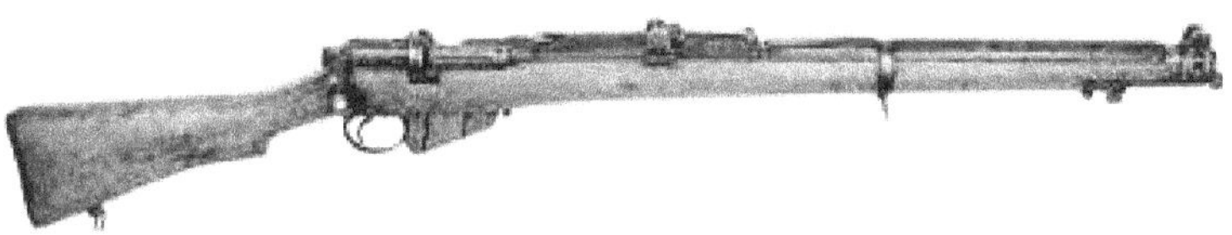

Lee-Enfield rifle, 303 caliber

Call signs for the American paratroopers
Lion 6 company commander
Tiger 6, first platoon leader on the company net
1-6 platoon ldr on the platoon net
1-1 first squad ldr, 1st platoon
1-2 second squad ldr, 1st platoon
1-3 third squad ldr, 1st platoon

Black Hornet recon drone

Postscript[3]

Eighty-three years after the rebellion against the British, the Battle of Samawah took place during the 2003 invasion of Iraq as American troops fought to clear the city of Iraqi forces. American paratroopers of the 82nd Airborne Division, with attached mechanized infantry and armor units, were given the task of clearing the city after it was bypassed during the dash to Baghdad. The battle was the largest sustained urban combat that paratroopers of the 82nd Airborne had been involved in since World War II.

To the present day, paratroopers from the 82nd Airborne have deployed to Iraq in the continuing campaign to secure the country.

---

[3] Wikipedia, last edited 16 January, 2024